This couldn't be happening to her, Kari thought.

Gage Reynolds had just walked back into her life. Right in the middle of a bank robbery... With a robber's gun pressed to her temple!

Eight years ago, Gage was her beloved, a young deputy, tall and handsome in his khaki uniform. He was still good-looking enough to make an angel want to sin. And now he was the sheriff of Possum Landing, judging by the badge on his shirt.

His dark eyes gleamed with interest at what he saw. "You know," he casually told the gunman, "that's Kari Asbury. The one who got away." He continued easily. "Eight years ago, that pretty lady there left me standing at the altar."

The bank robber glared at her. "That wasn't very nice. You want me to shoot her, Sheriff?"

Gage shrugged. "That's mighty neighborly of you...but I think I'd rather deal with her in my own way."

Kari gasped. Obviously, coming back to placid Possum Landing was going to be a whole lot more complicated than she'd thought....

Dear Reader,

A rewarding part of any woman's life is talking with friends about important issues. Because of this, we've developed the Readers' Ring, a book club that facilitates discussions of love, life and family. Of course, you'll find all of these topics wrapped up in each Silhouette Special Edition novel! Our featured author for this month's Readers' Ring is newcomer Elissa Ambrose. *Journey of the Heart* (#1506) is a poignant story of true love and survival when the odds are against you. This is a five-tissue story you won't be able to put down!

Susan Mallery delights us with another tale from her HOMETOWN HEARTBREAKERS series. *Good Husband Material* (#1501) begins with two star-crossed lovers and an ill-fated wedding. Years later, they realize their love is as strong as ever! Don't wait to pick up *Cattleman's Honor* (#1502), the second book in Pamela Toth's WINCHESTER BRIDES series. In this book, a divorced single mom comes to Colorado to start a new life—and winds up falling into the arms of a rugged rancher. What a way to go!

Victoria Pade begins her new series, BABY TIMES THREE, with a heartfelt look at unexpected romance, in *Her Baby Secret* (#1503)—in which an independent woman wants to have a child, and after a night of wicked passion with a handsome businessman, her wish comes true! You'll see that there's more than one way to start a family in Christine Flynn's *Suddenly Family* (#1504), in which two single parents who are wary of love find it—with each other! And you'll want to learn the facts in *What a Woman Wants* (#1505), by Tori Carrington. In this tantalizing tale, a beautiful widow discovers she's pregnant with her late husband's best friend's baby!

As you can see, we have nights of passion, reunion romances, babies and heart-thumping emotion packed into each of these special stories from Silhouette Special Edition.

Happy reading!

Karen Taylor Richman
Senior Editor

Please address questions and book requests to:
Silhouette Reader Service
U.S.: 3010 Walden Ave., P.O. Box 1325, Buffalo, NY 14269
Canadian: P.O. Box 609, Fort Erie, Ont. L2A 5X3

Susan Mallery

GOOD HUSBAND MATERIAL

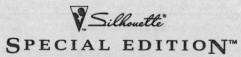

SPECIAL EDITION™

Published by Silhouette Books

America's Publisher of Contemporary Romance

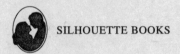 SILHOUETTE BOOKS

ISBN 0-373-24501-7

GOOD HUSBAND MATERIAL

Copyright © 2002 by Susan Macias Redmond

All rights reserved. Except for use in any review, the reproduction or utilization of this work in whole or in part in any form by any electronic, mechanical or other means, now known or hereafter invented, including xerography, photocopying and recording, or in any information storage or retrieval system, is forbidden without the written permission of the editorial office, Silhouette Books, 300 East 42nd Street, New York, NY 10017 U.S.A.

All characters in this book have no existence outside the imagination of the author and have no relation whatsoever to anyone bearing the same name or names. They are not even distantly inspired by any individual known or unknown to the author, and all incidents are pure invention.

This edition published by arrangement with Harlequin Books S.A.

® and TM are trademarks of Harlequin Books S.A., used under license. Trademarks indicated with ® are registered in the United States Patent and Trademark Office, the Canadian Trade Marks Office and in other countries.

Visit Silhouette at www.eHarlequin.com

Printed in U.S.A.

Books by Susan Mallery

SUSAN MALLERY

is the bestselling author of nearly fifty books for Harlequin and Silhouette Books. She makes her home in the Pacific Northwest with her handsome prince of a husband and her two adorable-but-not-bright cats.

Dear Reader,

What is it about old friends? It doesn't seem to matter how much time passes or what changes there have been in our lives—being with old friends renews the spirit, while reminding us of where we used to be and how far we've come.

Some of my book characters are like old friends—scary but true. ☺ One of my most successful series at Silhouette Special Edition features the Haynes family—four brothers, a half sister and a close friend. Over the course of six books, they each met their perfect match, fell in love and reaffirmed the bonds of family and marriage. I hated to say goodbye to them. Almost as soon as I finished the last book, I had the idea of going back to them someday.

That day is here. Welcome to my HOMETOWN HEARTBREAKERS, part two. If you are new to the series, don't worry. These books stand alone. If you are a fan of HOMETOWN HEARTBREAKERS, then I hope you will enjoy visiting old friends, while making new ones.

Two sets of brothers are about to have their worlds changed forever. They will find out they are not who they thought they were and begin a journey of self-discovery that will lead to love and a family they knew nothing about. Like the other Haynes men, these men respect the rules of the land and risk their lives to enforce them. They are heroes in the truest sense of the word.

These books are special to me, and I hope you will find the stories touch your heart, as well.

Best,

Susan Mallery

Chapter One

Kari Asbury fully expected to have trouble cashing her out-of-state check, she just didn't think she would have to put her life on the line to do it.

It wasn't just that the check was drawn from a bank in big, bad New York City; it was that her driver's license was also from that East Coast state. Ida Mae Montel would want to know why a girl born and raised in Possum Landing, Texas, would willingly run off to a place like that...a place with *Yankees*. And if a girl had to do such a thing, why on earth would she give up her Texas driver's license? Didn't everyone want to be from the Lone Star State?

No doubt Sue Ellen Boudine, the bank manager, would mosey on over to examine the check, all the while holding it like it was attached to a poisonous snake. They'd make a few calls (probably to friends, letting them know that Kari was back in town and with a New York driver's license, of all things), they'd hem and haw, and sigh heavily. Then they'd give Kari the money. Oh, but first they'd try to talk her into opening an account right there at the First Bank of Possum Landing.

Kari hesitated in front of the double glass doors, trying to figure out if she really needed the cash that badly. Maybe it would be better to pay the service fee and get the money out of the ATM machine. Then she reminded herself that the quicker everyone realized she'd returned to town for a very *temporary* visit, the quicker all the questions would be asked and answered. Then maybe she could have a little peace. Maybe.

There was the added thrill of finding out if Ida Mae still wore her hair in a beehive. How much hair spray did that upswept style require? Kari knew for a fact that Ida Mae only had her hair done once a week, yet it looked exactly the same on day seven as it did on day one.

Still smiling at the memory of Ida Mae's coiffure, she pulled open the door and stepped inside. She paused just past the threshold and waited for the shrieks of welcome and the group hug that would follow.

Nothing happened.

Kari frowned. She glanced around at the bank— established in 1892—taking in the tall, narrow windows, the real wood counters and stylish paneling. Ida Mae was in her regular spot—the first position on the left—as befitted the head teller. But the older woman wasn't talking. She wasn't even smiling. Her small eyes widened with something that looked like panic, and she made an odd gesture with her hand.

Before Kari could figure out what it meant, something hard and cold pressed against her cheek.

"Well, lookee here. We got us another customer, boys. At least this one's young and pretty. What my mama used to call a tall drink of water. That's something."

Kari's heart stopped. It might be nearly ninety in the shade outside, but here in the bank it felt closer to absolute zero.

Slowly, very slowly, she turned toward the man, who was holding a gun. He was short, stocky and wearing a ski mask. What on earth was going on?

"We're robbin' the bank," the man said, as if he could read her mind.

His astuteness startled her, until she realized his deduction wasn't much of a stretch.

She quickly glanced around. There were four of them, counting the man holding a gun on her. Two kept all the customers and most of the employees together at the far end of the bank, while the last one was behind the counter, putting money that Ida Mae handed him into a bag.

"You go ahead and set your purse on the floor," the man in front of her said. "Then start walking toward the other ladies. Do what you're told and no one will get hurt."

Kari flexed her hands slightly. Her chest tightened,

and it was nearly impossible to speak. "I, uh, I don't have a purse."

She didn't. She'd come into the bank with a check and her driver's license. Both were in the back pocket of her shorts.

The robber stared at her for a couple of seconds, then nodded. "Seems you don't. Now head on over there."

This couldn't be happening, Kari thought, even as she headed for the cluster of other customers huddled by the far end of the counter.

She was halfway to the safety of that crowd when the rear door of the bank opened.

"Well, hell," a low voice drawled. "One of us has bad timing, boys. You think it's you or me?"

Several women screamed. One of the masked men by the crowd grabbed an older woman and held the gun to her head. "Stay back," he yelled. "Stay back or the old lady dies."

Kari didn't have time to react. The man who had first held a gun to her jerked her arm to drag her back to him. She felt the pressure of the pistol against her cheek again. He wrapped one wiry arm around her neck, keeping her securely in place.

"Seems to me we've got a problem," the man holding her said. "So, Sheriff, why don't you just back out real slow and no one will get hurt."

The sheriff in question gave a sigh of the long-suffering. "I wish I could do that. But I can't. Want to know why?"

Kari felt as if she'd slipped into an alternative universe. This couldn't be happening to her. One second she'd been too scared to breathe, and the next, Gage Reynolds had walked back into her life. Right in the middle of a holdup.

Eight years ago he'd been a young deputy, tall and handsome in his khaki uniform. He was still good-looking enough to make an angel want to sin. He was also the sheriff, if the gleaming badge on his shirt pocket was to be believed. But for a man of the law, he didn't seem all that interested in the robbery going on right in front of him.

He took off his dust-colored cowboy hat and slapped it against his thigh. His dark hair gleamed, as did the interest in his eyes.

"Don't make me kill her," the gunman said, his tone low and controlled.

"You know who you've got there, son?" Gage asked casually, almost as if he hadn't figured out what was going on in the bank. "That's Kari Asbury."

"Back off, Sheriff."

The robber pressed the gun in a little deeper. Kari winced. Gage didn't seem to notice.

"She's the one who got away."

Kari could smell the criminal's sweat. She was willing to bet he hadn't planned on a hostage situation, and the fact he might be in over his head didn't make her breathe any easier. What on earth was Gage going on about?

"That's right," Gage continued, setting his hat on a table and stretching. "Eight years ago, that pretty lady there left me standing at the altar."

Despite the gun jammed into her cheek, Kari spluttered with indignation. "I did *not* leave you standing at the altar. We weren't even engaged."

"Maybe. But you knew I was gonna ask, and you took off. That's practically the same thing. Don't you think?"

He asked the last question of the robber, who actually considered before replying.

"If you hadn't really proposed, then she didn't leave you at the altar."

"Fair enough, but she *did* stand me up for the prom."

Kari couldn't believe it. Except for her grandmother's funeral seven years ago, she hadn't seen Gage since the afternoon of her high school prom. While she'd known that Possum Landing was small enough that they would eventually run into each other again, this wasn't exactly what she'd had in mind.

"It was complicated," she said, unable to believe she was being forced to defend herself in front of bank robbers.

"Did you or did you not skip town without warning? You left nothing but a note, Kari. You played with my heart like it was a football."

The bank robber glared at her. "That wasn't very nice."

She glared right back. "I was eighteen years old, okay? I apologized in the note."

"I've never gotten over it," Gage said, emotional pain oozing from every pore. He reached into his breast pocket and pulled out a package of gum. "You see before you a broken man."

Kari resisted the urge to roll her eyes. She didn't

know what Gage's game was, but she wished he would play it with someone else.

Her confusion turned to outrage when Gage took a stick of gum for himself, then offered the pack to the bank robber. Next they would be going out for a beer together.

Gage watched the anger flash in Kari's eyes. If she could have spit fire, he would be a scorched stick figure right about now. In different circumstances, Gage might have worried the issue, but not now.

The gunman shook off the gum, but that wasn't important. The gesture had been made and well received. Gage had established rapport.

"She went on up to New York City," Gage continued, tucking the gum package back into his breast pocket. "Wanted to be a fashion model."

The robber studied Kari, then shrugged. "She's pretty enough, but if she's back, then she didn't make it."

Gage sighed heavily again. "I guess not. All that pain and suffering for nothing."

Kari stiffened at his words, but didn't try to break away. Gage willed her to cooperate for just a few more seconds. While every instinct in his body screamed at him to jerk her free of the gunman, he forced himself to stay relaxed and focused. There were more people to protect than just Kari. Between the bank employees and the customers there were fifteen innocent citizens within the old walls. Fifteen unprepared folk and four men with guns. Gage didn't like the odds.

Using his peripheral vision, he checked on the

progress of the tactical team circling around the building. Just another minute or two and they would be in place.

"You want me to shoot her?" the gunman asked.

Kari gasped. Her big blue eyes widened even more, and the color drained from her face.

Gage chewed his gum for a second, then shrugged. "You know, that's mighty neighborly of you, but I think I'd rather deal with her in my own way, in my own time."

The team was nearly in place. Gage's heart was about to jump out of his chest, but he gave no outward sign. Another few seconds, he thought. Another—

"Hey, look!"

One of the robbers near the back turned suddenly. Everyone looked. A tactical team member dropped out of sight a moment too late. The gunman holding Kari snarled in rage.

"Dammit all to hell and back."

But that's all he got to say.

Gage lunged forward. He jerked Kari free, yelled at her to get down on the floor, then planted a booted foot firmly in the robber's midsection.

The bad guy gave a yelp of dismay as all the air rushed out of his lungs and he fell flat on his ass. He scooted a couple of feet backward, but by the time he sucked in a breath, two armed tactical team members had guns on him.

But they weren't as quick to capture the man by Ida Mae. A gunshot exploded.

Gage reacted without thinking. He turned and threw himself over Kari, covering her body with his.

A half-dozen or so rounds were fired. He pulled out his sidearm, looking for targets, and kept his free arm over Kari's face.

"Don't move," he growled in her ear.

"I can't," she gasped back.

After what felt like a lifetime, but was probably just seconds, a man called out. "I give, I give. You shot me."

There were muffled sounds, then a steady voice yelled, "Clear."

Five more "clear"s followed. Gage rolled off Kari and glanced around to check on the town folk. Everyone was fine—even Ida Mae, who had kicked the wounded gunman after she climbed to her feet. The leader of the tactical team walked over and stared down at Gage. He was covered in black from head to toe, with a visor over his face and enough firepower to take Cuba.

"I can't figure out if you were a damn fool or especially brave for walking in on a bank robbery in progress," the man said.

Gage sat up and grinned. "Someone had to do it, and I figured none of your boys was going to volunteer. Plus we know these were small-town criminals. They're used to seeing someone like me around. One of you all dressed in the Darth Vader clothes would have scared 'em into acting like fools. Someone could have gotten killed."

The man nodded. "If you ever get tired of small-town life, you'd be a fine addition to our team."

Gage didn't even consider his offer. "I'm flat-tered,'' he said easily, ''but I'm right where I want to be.''

The man nodded and walked off.

''You knew they were there.''

He turned and saw Kari staring at him. She still lay on the ground. Her once long blond hair had been cut short and stylish. Makeup accentuated her already big, beautiful blue eyes. Time had sculpted her face into something even more lovely than he remembered.

''The tactical team?'' he asked. ''Sure. They were circling the building.''

''So I wasn't in danger?''

''Kari, a criminal was holding a gun to your head. I wouldn't say that ever qualifies as safe.''

She smiled then. A slow, sexy smile that he still remembered. Lordy but she'd been a looker back then. Time hadn't changed that.

He suddenly became aware of the adrenaline pouring through his body. And the fact that he hadn't had sex in far too long. Eight years ago, he and Kari had never gotten around to that particular pleasure. He wondered if she would be more open to the experience now.

He got to his feet. If she was back in Possum Landing for any length of time, he would be sure to find out.

''Welcome back,'' he said, and held out his hand to help her up.

She placed her fingers against his palm. ''Jeez, Gage, if you wanted to find a unique way to welcome me home, couldn't you just have held a parade?''

* * *

"You can go now, Ms. Asbury," the wiry detective said nearly four hours later.

Kari sighed in relief. She'd given her statement, been questioned, been fed and watered, and now she was finally free to head home. As far as she could tell, there were only a couple of problems. The first was that her heart refused to return to normal. Every time she thought about what had happened in the bank, her chest felt as if it were filled with thundering horse hooves. The second problem was that she had walked to the bank, a scant mile or so from her house, but the sheriff's station was clear on the other side of town. It was summer in the middle of Texas, which meant billion-degree heat and humidity to match.

"Do you think I could have a ride home?" she asked. "Or is Willy still running a cab around these parts?"

The detective gave her a once-over, then grinned. "Wish I could take you home myself. Unfortunately I have more work to do. I'll get one of the deputies to take you."

Kari smiled her thanks. When she was alone, she glanced out of the glass-enclosed office. Just looking around, she told herself. She wasn't actually looking for someone specific. Certainly not Gage.

But like a bee heading for the sweetest flower, she found herself settling her gaze on him. He was across the large office, still in a glass room of his own, chatting with some members of the federal tactical team. Were they trying to talk him into leaving Possum Landing to join them? Kari shook her head. She might have been gone for eight years, but some things never changed. Gage Reynolds would no more leave Possum Landing than NASA would send Ida Mae up in the next space shuttle.

She watched as Gage spoke and the other men laughed. Time had honed him into a hard man, she thought. Hard in a good way—with thick muscles and a steady set to his face. Despite the fact that she'd been there when it happened, she couldn't believe that he'd actually walked into a bank robbery. On purpose! He'd been calm and cool and he'd about made her crazy.

The detective strolled back into the office. "Ms. Asbury, if you'll wait by the front desk, the deputy will be with you in a couple of minutes."

She smiled her thanks and followed him out to the waiting area. Ida Mae sat there, her hands folded primly on her lap. When she saw Kari, her wrinkled face broke out into a welcoming smile.

"Kari."

The older woman rose and held out her arms. Kari moved forward and accepted the hug. Everything about it was familiar—Ida Mae's bony arms, her beehive hairdo with not a hair out of place, the scent of the gardenia perfume she always wore.

"You're looking fine, child," Ida Mae said as she released Kari and sank back onto the bench.

Kari settled next to her. "You haven't changed a bit," she said, then patted her hand. "Are you all right?"

Ida Mae touched her chest. "I thought I was gonna have a heart attack right there in the middle of the bank. I couldn't believe my own eyes when those boys pulled guns on us. Then you walked in and it was like seeing a ghost. And then Gage strolled in. Wasn't he brave?''

"Absolutely," Kari agreed. She wasn't sure she could have knowingly walked in on a bank robbery, regardless of who was at risk. But Gage had always believed in doing what was right.

Ida Mae gave her a knowing look. "He's still a handsome devil, too, don't you think? Is he taller than when you left?''

Kari wanted to roll her eyes, but figured she was getting a little old for that particular response. Fortunately, Ida Mae was on a tear and didn't require an answer.

"No one knew you were coming back," the older woman said. "Of course, we knew you'd have to eventually, what with you still owning your grandma's house and all. I can tell you, tongues wagged when you left town all those years ago. Poor Gage. You about broke his heart. Of course, you were young and you had to follow your dreams. It's just too bad that your dreams didn't include him.''

Kari didn't know what to say. Her heart had been broken, too, but she didn't want to get into that. The past was the past. At least, that's what she told herself, even though she didn't actually believe it.

Ida Mae smiled. "It's good that you're back.''

Kari sighed softly. "Ida Mae, I'm not back. I'm just here for the summer.'' Then she was going to shake the dust from this small town off her shoes and never look back.

"Uh-huh." Ida Mae didn't look convinced.

Fortunately the deputy arrived just then. Kari asked Ida Mae if she needed a ride home, as well.

"No, no. My Nelson is probably waiting out front for me. I called him just before you walked out."

Led by the deputy, they headed out the front door and down the three steps to the sidewalk. By the time she saw that Nelson was indeed waiting for his wife, Kari had broken out into a sweat and was having trouble breathing in the heat.

"Little Kari Asbury," Nelson said as he approached. He grinned at her as he mopped his forehead with a handkerchief. "You're all grown up."

Kari smiled.

"Didn't she turn out pretty?" Ida Mae said fondly. "But then, you were always a lovely girl. You should have entered the Miss Texas pageant. You could have gone far with a title like that."

Kari smiled weakly. "It was very nice to see you both," she said politely, then headed toward the squad car that the deputy had pulled around.

"Gage has had a couple of close calls," Nelson called after her, "but no one's gotten him down the aisle."

Kari waved by way of response. She wasn't going to touch that particular topic.

"Good to have you back," Nelson yelled louder.

This one Kari couldn't resist. She turned toward the older man and shook her head. "I'm not back."

Nelson only waved.

"Just perfect," she muttered as she climbed into the car with the deputy. He'd told her his name, but she'd already forgotten it. Probably because he looked so impossibly young. She was only twenty-six, but next to this guy she felt ancient.

She gave him her address and leaned back against the seat, breathing in the air-conditioned coolness. There were a thousand and one details to occupy her mind, yet instead of dealing with them, she found herself remembering the first time she'd met Gage. She'd been all of seventeen and he'd been twenty-three. At the time, he'd seemed so much older and more mature.

"I know this is a crazy question," she said, glancing at the young man next to her. "But how old are you?"

He was blond, with blue eyes and pale cheeks. He gave her a startled glance. "Twenty-three."

"Oh."

The same age Gage had been eight years ago. That didn't seem possible. If Gage had been as young as this guy, Kari shouldn't have had any trouble standing up to him. Why had she found it so incredibly difficult to share her feelings while they'd been dating? Why had the thought of telling him the truth terrified her?

There wasn't an easy answer to the question, and before she could come up with a hard one, they arrived at her house.

Kari thanked the deputy and stepped out into the late afternoon. In front of her stood the old house where she'd grown up. It had been built in the forties, and had a wide porch and gabled windows. Different colored versions of the same house sat all along the street, including the home next door. She glanced at it, wondering when she would have her next run-in with her neighbor. As if returning to Possum Landing for the summer wasn't complicated enough, Gage Reynolds now lived next door.

Kari walked inside her grandmother's house and stood in the main parlor. Never a living room, she thought with a smile. It was a parlor, where people "set" when it wasn't nice enough to settle on the front porch. She remembered countless hours spent listening to her grandmother's friends talking about everything from who was pregnant to who was cheating on whom.

She'd arrived after dark last night. She hadn't turned on many lights after she'd come in, and somehow she'd convinced herself that the house was different. Only now, she saw it wasn't.

The old sofas were the same, as was the horsehair chair her grandmother had inherited from *her* grandmother. Kari had always hated that piece—it was both slick and uncomfortable. Now she touched the antique and felt the memories wash over her.

Maybe it was the result of all the emotions from the robbery, maybe it was just the reality of being home. Either way, she suddenly sensed the ghosts in the house. At least they were friendly, she told herself as she moved into the old kitchen. Her grandmother had always loved her.

Kari looked at the pecan cabinets and the stove and oven unit that had to be at least thirty years old. If she expected to get a decent price for the old place, she would have to do some serious updating. That was the reason she'd come home for the summer, after all.

A restlessness filled her. She hurried upstairs and changed out of her clothes. After showering, she slipped on a cotton dress and padded back downstairs barefoot. She toured the house, almost as if she were waiting for something to happen.

And then it did.

There was a knock on the door. She didn't have to answer it to know who had come calling. Her stomach lurched and her heart took up that thundering hoof dance again. She drew in a deep breath and reached for the handle.

Chapter Two

Gage stood on Kari's front porch. She didn't bother pretending to be surprised. Her time with him in the bank had been too rushed and too emotionally charged for her to notice much about his appearance…and how he might have changed. But now that they were in a more normal situation, she could take the time to appreciate how he'd filled out in the years she'd been away.

He looked taller than she remembered. Or maybe he was just bigger. Regardless, he was very much a man now. Still too good-looking for her peace of mind. He appealed to her, but, then, he always had.

"If you're inviting me to attend another bank robbery," she said with a smile, "I'm going to have to pass."

Gage grinned and held up both hands. "No more crime…not if I can prevent it." He leaned against the door frame. "The reason I stopped by was to make sure that you were all right after all the excitement today. Plus, I knew you'd want to thank me for saving your life by inviting me to dinner."

She tilted her head as she considered him. "What if my husband objects?"

He didn't even have the grace to look the least bit worried. "You're not married. Ida Mae keeps track of these things, and she would have told me."

"Figures." She stepped back to allow him inside. Gage moved into the front room while she closed the door behind him. "What makes you think I've had time to go to the grocery store?" she asked.

"If you haven't, I have a couple of steaks in the freezer. I could get those out."

She shook her head. "Actually, I did my shopping this morning. That's the reason I ran out of cash and had to go get more at the bank." She frowned. "Come to think of it, I never did cash that check."

"You can do it tomorrow."

"I guess I'll have to."

She led the way into the kitchen. Having him here was strange, she thought. An odd blending of past and present. How many times had he come over for dinner eight years ago? Her grandmother had always welcomed him at their table. Kari had been so in love that she'd been thrilled he'd wanted to spend mealtimes with her. Of course, she'd been young enough to be excited even if all he wanted was for her to keep him company while he washed his car. All she'd needed to be happy was a few hours in Gage's presence. Life had been a whole lot simpler in those days.

He leaned against a counter and sniffed. "That smells mighty good. And familiar."

"Grandmother's sauce recipe. I put it in the slow cooker this morning, right after I got back from the grocery store. I also got out the old bread maker, but as it's been gathering dust forever, I can't promise it'll all work."

His dark gaze settled on her. "It works just fine."

His words made her break out in goose bumps, which was crazy. He was a smooth-talking good-ol' boy from Possum Landing. She lived in New York City. No way Gage Reynolds should be able to get to her. And he didn't. Not really.

"Did you get all the paperwork wrapped up, or whatever it was you had to do after the robbery?" she asked as she checked on the pasta sauce.

"Everything is tied up in a neat package." He crossed to the kitchen table and picked up the bottle of wine she'd left there.

"Kari Asbury, is this liquor? Have you brought the devil's brew into our saintly dry county?"

She glanced up and chuckled. "You know it. I remembered there weren't any liquor sales allowed around here and figured I had better bring my own. I stopped on my way over from the airport."

"I'm shocked. Completely shocked."

She grinned. "So you probably don't want to know that there's beer in the refrigerator."

"Not at all." He opened the door and pulled out a bottle. When he offered it to her, she shook her head.

"I'll wait for wine with dinner."

He opened the drawer with the bottle opener in it on the first try. Gage moved around with the ease of someone familiar with the place. But then, he *had* been. He'd moved in next door, the spring before her senior year. She remembered watching him carry in boxes and pieces of furniture. Her grandmother had told her who he was—the new deputy. Gage Reynolds. He'd been in the army and had traveled the world. To her seventeen-year-old eyes, a young man of twenty-three had seemed impossibly grown-up and mature. When they'd started dating that fall, he'd seemed a man of the world and she'd been—

"Are we still neighbors?" she asked, turning back to face him.

"I'm still next door."

She thought of Ida Mae's comment that Gage had never made it to the altar. Somehow he'd managed to not get caught. Looking at him now, his khaki uniform emphasizing the breadth of his shoulders and the muscles in his legs, she wondered how the lovely ladies of Possum Landing had managed to keep from trapping him.

Not her business, she reminded herself. She checked the timer on the bread machine and saw there was still fifteen minutes to go, plus cooling time.

"Let's go into the parlor," she said. "We'll be more comfortable."

He nodded and led the way.

As she followed him, she found her gaze drifting lower, to his rear. She nearly stumbled in shock. What on earth was wrong with her? She didn't ever stare at men's butts. Nothing about them had ever seemed overly interesting. Until now.

She sighed. Obviously, living next door to Gage was going to be more complicated than she'd realized.

He settled into a wing chair, while she took the sofa. Gage drank some of his beer, then put the bottle on a crocheted coaster and leaned back. He should have looked awkward and out of place in this fussy, feminine room, but he didn't. Perhaps because he'd always been comfortable anywhere.

"What are you thinking?" he asked.

"That you look at home in my grandmother's house."

"I spent a lot of time here," he reminded her. "Even after you left, she and I stayed close."

She didn't want to think about that...about the confidences that might have been shared.

Gage studied her face. "You've changed."

She wasn't sure if he meant the comment in a good way or a bad way. "It's been a long time."

"I never thought you'd come back."

It was the second time in less than three hours that someone had mentioned her being back. "I'm not back," she clarified. "At least, not for anything permanent."

Gage didn't look surprised by her statement, nor did he seem to take issue with her defensive tone. "So why are you suddenly here? It's been seven years since your grandmother died."

Her temper faded as quickly as it had flared. She

sighed. "I want to fix up the house so I can sell it. I'm just here for the summer while I do that."

He nodded without saying anything. She had the uncomfortable sense of having been judged and found wanting. Which wasn't fair. Gage wasn't the type of man to judge people without just cause. So her need to squirm in her seat had nothing to do with him and everything to do with her own state of mind.

Rather than deal with personal inadequacies that were probably better left unexplored in public, she changed the subject. "I can't believe there was a bank robbery right here in Possum Landing. It's going to be the talk of the town for weeks."

"Probably. But it wasn't that much of a surprise."

"I can't believe that. Things couldn't have changed that much."

He nodded. "We're still just a bump in the road, with plenty of small-town problems, but nothing even close to big-city crime. These boys were working their way across the state, robbing hometown banks. I'd been keeping track of their progress, figuring they'd get here sooner or later. Four days ago, the feds came calling. They wanted to set up a sting. I didn't have a problem with that. We talked to everyone at the bank, marked a drawer full of money, then waited for the hit to take place."

Kari couldn't believe it. "All that excitement right here, and I was in the thick of it."

Gage narrowed his eyes. "As you saw, things got out of hand. I don't know if those robbers got lazy or cocky, but this time, they decided to hold up the bank while there were still customers inside. Previously they'd waited until just before the doors were locked for the day, to go in.''

''So you weren't expecting to deal with a hostage situation?''

''No one was. The feds wanted to wait it out, but those were my people inside. Someone had to do something.''

She turned that thought over in her mind. ''So you just waltzed inside to distract them?''

''It seemed like the easiest way to get the job done. Plus, I wanted to be there to make sure no one went crazy and got shot. At least, no one from here. I don't much care about the criminals.''

Of course. In Gage's mind, they had brought the situation upon themselves. He wouldn't take responsibility for their coming to Possum Landing to hold up a bank in the first place.

''I have to agree with the federal officer,'' she said. ''I don't know if you were brave or stupid.''

He smiled. ''You could probably make a case for either point of view.'' He took another drink of his beer. ''You know that I wasn't really mad at you. I was trying to distract that one guy so he didn't take you hostage.''

She shivered at the memory of the gun held to her head. ''It took me a few minutes to catch on to what you were doing.''

But that didn't stop her from wondering how much of what he had said was true. Did Gage really think she was the one who got away?

Did she want to be?

Once she easily would have said yes. Back before

she'd left town, Gage had been her entire world. She would have thrown herself in front of a moving train if he'd asked. She'd loved him with all the crazy devotion a teenager was capable of. That had been the trouble—she'd loved him too much. When she'd figured out there were problems, she hadn't known how to deal with them. So she'd run. When he hadn't come after her, he'd confirmed her greatest fear in the world…that he hadn't loved her at all.

They spent all of dinner talking about mutual friends. Gage brought her up to date on various weddings, divorces and births.

"I can't believe Sally has twins," Kari said, as they moved to the porch and sat on the wooden swing.

"Two girls. I told Bob he has his work cut out for him once they become teenagers."

"Fortunately that's a long way off."

Kari set her glass of wine on the dusty, peeling table beside the swing and leaned back to look up at the sky. It might be after dark, but it was still plenty hot and humid. She could feel her dress sticking to her skin. Her head felt funny—fuzzy, heavy and more than a little out of sync. No doubt it was due to the combination of the fear she'd experienced earlier in the day and a little too much wine with dinner. She didn't normally allow herself more than half a glass on special occasions, but tonight she and Gage had nearly split the bottle.

Gage stretched out his long legs. He didn't seem bothered by the wine. No doubt his additional body mass helped, not to mention the fact that he wouldn't have spent the past several years trying to maintain an unnaturally thin body.

"Tell me about life in New York," he said.

"There isn't much to tell," she admitted, wondering if she should be pleased or worried that he'd finally asked her a vaguely personal question. "When I arrived, I found out that small-town girls who had been told they were pretty enough to be a model were spilling out of every modeling agency within a thirty-mile radius. The competition was tough and the odds of making it into the big time were close to zero."

"You did okay."

She glanced at him, not sure if he was assuming or if he actually knew. "After the first year or so, I got work. Eventually I made enough to support myself and pay for college. As of last month, I have teaching credentials, which is what I always wanted."

Gage glanced at her. "You're still too skinny to be a PE teacher."

She laughed. "I know. I sure won't miss all those years of dieting. I'm proud to tell you that I've worked my way up from a size two to a six. My goal is to be a size ten and even eat chocolate now and then."

He swept his gaze over her. She half expected a comment on her body, but instead he only asked, "So what kind of teacher are you?"

"Math at the middle-school level," she said.

"A lot of those boys are going to have a crush on you."

"They'll get over it."

"I don't know. I still get a hankering for Ms. Rosens. She taught eighth grade social studies. I don't think I'd bothered to notice girls before. Then she walked into the room and I was a goner. She married the high school football coach. It took me a year to get over it."

She laughed.

They rocked in silence for a few minutes. Life was so normal here, Kari thought, enjoying the quiet of the evening. Instead of sirens and tire screeches, there were only the calls of the night critters. All around Possum Landing people would be out on their porches, enjoying the stars and visiting with neighbors. No one would worry about half a glass of wine causing facial puffiness, or being too bloated for a lingerie shoot. No one would lose a job for gaining three pounds.

This was normal, she reminded herself. She'd nearly been gone long enough to forget what that was like.

"Why teaching?" Gage asked unexpectedly.

"It's what I always wanted."

"After the modeling."

"Right."

She didn't want to go there—not now. Maybe later they would rehash their past and hurl accusations at each other, but not tonight.

"Where are you applying?"

"To schools around Texas. There are a couple of openings in the Dallas area and in Abilene. I have some interviews scheduled. That's why this seemed like the perfect time to come back and fix up the house. Then I can move on."

She paused, expecting him to respond. But he didn't.

Which was just as well, because she suddenly found that sitting next to him on the old swing where he'd kissed her for the first time was more difficult than she would have thought. Her chest felt tight and her skin tingled all over.

It was just the wine, she told herself. Or it was the old memories, swimming around them like so many ghosts. The past was a powerful influence. No doubt she would need a little time to get used to being back in Possum Landing.

"Did you apply locally?" Gage asked.

"No."

She waited, but he didn't ask why.

"Enough about me," she said, shifting in her seat and angling toward him. "What about your life? Last I heard, you were still a deputy. When did you run for sheriff?"

"Last year. I wasn't sure I'd make it my first time out, but I did."

She wasn't surprised. Gage had always been good at his job and well liked by the community. "So you got what you always wanted."

"Uh-huh." He glanced at her. "I was always real clear about my goals. I grew up here. I'm a fifth-generation resident of Possum Landing. I knew I wanted to see the world, then come back home and make my life here. So I did."

She admired his ability to know what he wanted and go after it. She had never been quite that focused.

There had been the occasional powerful distraction. One of them was sitting right next to her.

"I'm glad you're where you want to be," she said. Then, because she wasn't always as bright as she looked, she said, "But you never married."

Gage smiled. "There have been a few close calls."

"You always were a favorite with the ladies."

His smile faded. "I never gave you cause to worry when we were together. I didn't fool around on you, Kari."

"I never thought you did." She shrugged. "But there were plenty of women eager to see if they could capture your attention. The fact that you and I were going out didn't seem to impress them."

"It impressed me."

His voice seemed to scrape along her skin like a rough caress. She shivered slightly.

"Yes, well, I..." Her voice trailed off. So much for being sophisticated, she thought wryly. Yup, her time in the big city had sure polished her.

"It's getting late," Gage said.

He rose, and she wasn't sure if she was sad or relieved that he was going. Part of her didn't want the evening to end, but another part of her was grateful that she wouldn't have another chance to say something stupid. As much as she'd grown and matured, she'd never quite been able to kick that particular habit.

She stood as well, noticing again how tall he was. Especially in his worn cowboy boots. Barefoot, he only had four inches on her. Now she had to tilt her head slightly to meet his gaze.

The look in his eyes nearly took her breath away. There was a combination of confidence and fire that made her insides sort of melt and her breathing turn ragged.

What on earth was wrong with her? She couldn't possibly be feeling anything like anticipation. That would be crazy. That would be—

"You're still the prettiest girl in Possum Landing," he said as he took a step toward her.

She suddenly felt overwhelmed by the Texas heat. "I, um, I'm not really a girl anymore."

He smiled a slow, easy, "I'm in charge here and don't you forget it" kind of smile that didn't do anything positive for her equilibrium. She seemed to have forgotten how to breathe.

"I know," he murmured as he put his hand on the back of her neck and drew her close. "Did I mention I like your hair short?"

She opened her mouth to answer. Big mistake. Or not, depending on one's point of view.

Because just at that moment, he lowered his mouth to hers. She didn't have time to prepare…which was probably a good thing. Because the second his lips touched hers, protesting seemed like a really silly idea—when Gage could kiss this good.

Kari wasn't exactly sure what he was doing that was so special. Sure there was soft, firm pressure and plenty of passion. As if the night wasn't warm enough, they were generating enough heat between them to boil water on contact. But there was something else, some chemistry that left her desperate and longing. Something that urged her to wrap her arms around him so that when he pulled her close, they were touching everywhere it mattered.

He moved his mouth against hers, then lightly licked her lower lip. Pleasure shot through her like lightning. She clutched at his strong shoulders, savoring the hardness of his body against hers, liking the feel of his hands on her hips and his chest flattening her breasts.

Her head tilted slightly, as did his, in preparation for the kiss to deepen. Because there wasn't a doubt in her mind that they were taking this to the next level.

So when he stroked her lower lip again, she parted her mouth for him. And when he slowly eased his tongue inside, she was ready and very willing to dance this particular dance.

He tasted sweet and sexy. He was a man who enjoyed women and knew enough to make sure they enjoyed him. Kari had a hazy recollection of her first kiss with Gage, when he'd been so sure and she'd felt like a dolt. Right up until he'd touched his tongue to hers and she'd melted like butter on a hot griddle.

Now that same trickling sensation started deep inside. Her body was more than ready for a trip down memory lane. She wasn't so sure the rest of her could play catch-up that fast...even if the passion threatened to overwhelm her.

He moved his hand up from her hips to her sides, then around to her back, moving higher and higher until he cupped her head. He slid his fingers into her short hair and softly whispered her name.

She continued to hold on to him because the alternative was to fall on her rear end right there on the porch. When he broke the kiss and began to nibble along the line of her jaw, she didn't care where she fell as long as he caught her. And when he sucked on her earlobe, every cell in her body screamed out that sex with Gage Reynolds would be a perfect homecoming.

Fortunately, the choice wasn't hers. Just when she was starting to think they were wearing too many layers, he stepped back. His eyes were bright, his mouth damp with their kisses. She was pleased to see that his breathing was a tad too fast and that parts of him were not as...modest as they had been a few moments before.

They stared at each other. Kari didn't know what to say. Finding out that Gage kissed better than she remembered meant one of three things: her memory was faulty, he'd been practicing while she'd been gone, or the chemistry between them was more powerful than it had been eight years ago. She wasn't sure which she wanted it to be.

He didn't speak, either. Instead, he leaned close, gave her one last hot, hard kiss, and walked down the porch steps, into the night.

Kari was left staring after him. Restlessness seized her, making her want to follow him and...and...

She sucked in a breath before slowly turning and heading back into the house. Obviously, coming back to Possum Landing was going to be a whole lot more complicated than she'd first realized.

Chapter Three

Gage ambled toward the offices of the *Possum Landing Gazette* the following morning. Under normal circumstances, he would have put off this meeting for as long as possible. But ever since the previous evening, he hadn't been able to concentrate on his work, so he figured this was a better use of his time than staring out the window and remembering.

He'd always known that Kari would come back to Possum Landing one day. He'd felt it in his bones. From time to time he'd considered what his reaction to that event would be, assuming he would be little more than mildly interested in how she'd changed and only slightly curious as to her future plans. He hadn't thought there would still be any chemistry between them. He wasn't sure if that made him a fool, or an optimist.

The chemistry was there in spades. As were a lot of old feelings he didn't want to acknowledge. Being around her made him remember what it was like to want her...and not just in bed. There had been a time when he'd longed to spend his whole life with her, making babies and creating a past they could both be proud of. Instead, she'd gone away and he'd found contentment in his present life. While the kiss the previous evening had shown him that parts of him were still very interested in the woman she'd become, the rest of him couldn't afford to be.

Kari was a beautiful woman. Wanting her in bed made sense. Expecting anything else would take him down a road he refused to travel. He'd been there once and he hadn't liked the destination.

So, for however long she stayed in Possum Landing, he would be a good neighbor and enjoy her company. If that led to something between the sheets, that was just fine with him. He hadn't had much interest in the fairer sex these past few months. Instead, a restlessness had seized him, making him want something he couldn't define. If nothing else, Kari could prove to be a welcome distraction.

Gage entered the newspaper office and nodded at the receptionist. "I know my way," he called as he headed down a long corridor. "I'd be obliged if you'd tell Daisy I'm here."

The woman picked up the phone to call back to the reporter. Gage pulled off his cowboy hat and slapped it against his thigh.

He didn't much want to be here, but experience had taught him that it was safer to show up for interviews than to allow Daisy to come to him. This way, he was in charge and could head out when he felt the need to escape. He'd figured out that by leaning against the conference room chairs just so, he could activate the test button on his pager. It went off, and he could glance down at the screen and pretend something had come up, forcing him to leave. He was also sure to seem real regretful about having to head out unexpectedly. He was just as sure to ignore Daisy's not-so-subtle hints that they should get together sometime soon.

Daisy was a fine figure of a woman. A petite redhead with big green eyes and a mouth that promised three kinds of heaven if a man were only to ask. They'd been in the same class in high school but had never dated. Newly divorced, Daisy was more than willing to reacquaint herself with Gage. He appreciated the compliment and couldn't for the life of him figure out why he wasn't interested. But he wasn't. As he'd yet to decide on an easy way to let her down, he did the next best thing and avoided anything personal.

He wove his way through the half dozen or so desks in the main room of the newspaper office. Daisy was in the back, by a window. She looked up and smiled as Gage approached. Her long, red hair had been piled on her head in a mass of sexy curls. The sleeveless blouse she wore dipped low enough to prove that her cleavage was God-given and not the result of padding. Her smile more than welcomed…it offered. Gage smiled in return, all the while monitoring parts south. Over the years he'd found that part of him was a fairly good judge of his interest in a woman. As had occurred every other time he'd been in Daisy's company, there wasn't even a hint of a stirring. No matter how much Daisy might wish the contrary, as far as he was concerned, there wasn't any future for them.

"Gage," she murmured as he approached. "You're looking fine this morning. Being a hero seems to agree with you."

"Daisy," he said with a smile. "If you're going to write anything about me being a hero in your article, I'm not going to cooperate. I was doing my job—nothing more."

She sighed and tilted her head. "Brave *and* modest. Two of my favorite qualities in a man." She batted her long lashes at him. "I have a call to make. Why don't you wait for me in the conference room, and I'll join you there."

"Sure thing."

He spoke easily, even though the last place he wanted Daisy to send him was that back room with no windows and only one door. Yesterday, facing four armed bank robbers hadn't done much but increase his heart rate. But the thought of being trapped in a small place with Daisy on the hunt made his insides shrivel up and play dead.

Still, there was no escaping the inevitable. And he always had his handy-dandy test button escape route.

He walked down the hallway that led to the conference room and stepped inside. But instead of finding it empty, he saw someone else waiting. A tall, slender someone with short blond hair and the prettiest blue eyes this side of the Mississippi.

"Morning, Kari," he said as he stepped into the room.

She glanced up from the list she'd been making, frowned in confusion, then smiled. "Gage. What are you doing here?"

"Waiting on Daisy. She's going to interview me about yesterday's bank robbery." He hesitated before taking a seat.

Some decisions were harder than others and this was one of them. Did he want to sit next to her so he could catch the occasional whiff of her soft perfume, or sit across from her so he could look at her lovely face? He decided to enjoy the view, and pulled out the chair directly opposite hers.

"What brings you to the newspaper this morning?" he asked as he set his hat on the table.

Kari's mouth twisted slightly. "Daisy called and asked to interview me about the bank robbery. I wonder why she wanted us to come at the same time."

Gage had a couple of ideas, but figured this wasn't the time to go into them. Instead he studied Kari, who seemed to be trying *not* to look at him. Was that because of last night? Their kiss? The heat they'd ignited had kept him up half the night. He might not have much of a reaction to Daisy, but being around Kari proved that he could be intrigued in about a tenth of a second under the right circumstances.

This morning she wore a white summery dress that emphasized her slender shape. He eyed her short hair, which fluttered around her ears.

"What?" she said, watching him watch her. She touched her hair. "I know—it's short."

"I said I liked it."

"I wasn't sure if you were lying," she admitted with a smile. "I always figured you were more of a long hair kind of a guy."

He leaned back in his chair. "Actually, I try to be flexible. If it looks nice, I like it."

He continued to take in her features, noting changes and similarities.

"What are you thinking?" she asked.

He grinned. He was thinking that he would very much like to take her to bed. Once they'd shared several hours of one of life's greatest pleasures, he would like to get to know the woman she'd become while she'd been gone. Not that he was going to say that to her. From time to time, circumstances forced a man to tell little white lies.

"I was wondering how much work you're planning on doing at your grandmother's house."

Kari blinked at Gage. She'd expected him to say a lot of things, but not that. He'd been looking at her as if he were the big bad wolf and she were lunch. But in the kind of way that made her body heat up and her heart rate slip into overdrive.

So, she'd been thinking about last night's kiss and he'd been mulling over paint chips and siding. Obviously her ability to read Gage and handle herself with grace and style hadn't improved at all in the time she'd been gone.

"I'm still figuring that out," she said. "The bi-weekly cleaning service kept the house livable, but it's still old and out of date. I could redo the whole place, but that doesn't make sense. I have a limit to both my time and money, so I'm going to have to prioritize.''

He nodded thoughtfully.

My, oh my, but he still looked good, she thought, as she had yesterday. And the pleasure she took in seeing him hadn't worn off yet. She wondered if it would. By the end of summer, would he be little more than just some good-looking guy who happened to live next door? Could she possibly get that lucky?

Before she could answer her own question, Daisy breezed into the conference room. From her low-cut blouse to the red lipstick emphasizing her full lips, she was a walking, breathing pinup girl. Kari felt bony and string-bean–like in comparison.

''Thanks so much for coming,'' she said as she closed the door, then took the seat next to Gage. ''I'm writing a follow-up article for the paper and I thought it would be fun to interview you both together. I hope you don't mind.''

Kari shook her head and tried not to notice how close Daisy sat to Gage. The other woman brushed her arm against his and smiled at him in a way that had Kari thinking they were way more than friends.

But that didn't make sense. Gage wasn't the kind of man to be involved with one woman and kiss another. Which meant Gage and Daisy had once been a couple or that they were still in the flirting stage. Either concept gave her the willies.

Daisy set her notebook on the table in front of her but didn't open it. She leaned toward Kari. ''Wasn't that something? I mean, a bank robbery right here in PL.''

Kari blinked. ''PL?''

''Possum Landing. Nothing exciting ever happens here.'' She smiled at Gage. ''At least, nothing in public. I thought it was so amazing. And, Gage, throwing yourself in front of the bullets. That was amazing, too. And brave.''

He grunted.

With a speed that left Kari scrambling, Daisy turned to her and changed the subject. ''So, you're back. After all those years in New York. What was it like there?''

''Interesting,'' Kari said cautiously, not sure what this had to do with the holdup the previous day. ''Different from here.''

''Isn't everywhere,'' Daisy said with a laugh. ''I've spent time in the city, but I have to tell you, I'm a small-town girl at heart. PL is an amazing place and has everything I could ever want.''

She spoke earnestly, focusing all her attention on Gage for several seconds before swinging it back on Kari.

''What's it like seeing Gage again after all these years?''

Kari blinked. ''I'm, uh, not sure what that has to do with the bank robbery.''

''I would have thought it was obvious. Your former fiancé risks his life for you. He protects you from the hail of gunfire. You can't tell me you didn't think it was romantic. Don't you think it was the perfect homecoming? I mean, now that you're back.''

Kari risked a glance at Gage, but he looked as confused as she felt. What on earth was Daisy's point with all this? As Kari didn't want anything she said taken out of context and printed for the whole town to see, she tried to think before she spoke.

"First of all," she said slowly, "Gage and I were never engaged. We dated. Second, I'm not back. Not permanently."

"Uh-huh." Daisy opened her notebook and scribbled a few lines. "Gage, what were you thinking when you walked into the bank?"

"That I should have followed my mama's advice and studied to be an engineer."

Kari smiled slightly and felt herself relax. Trust Gage to ease the tension in the room. But before she could savor her newfound peace, Daisy broke into peals of laughter, tossing her pen on the table and clutching Gage's arm.

"Aren't you a hoot?" she said, beaming at him. "I've always enjoyed your humor."

The expression on her face said she had enjoyed other things, as well, but Kari didn't want to dwell on that. She tried to ignore the couple across the table. Daisy wasn't having any of that. She turned her attention back to Kari and gave her a look of friendly concern.

"I'm so pleased to hear you say that you're not staying for the long haul. You and Gage had something special once, but I've found that old flames never light up as brightly the second time around. They seem to fizzle and just fade away."

Kari smiled through clenched teeth. "Well, bless your heart for being so concerned."

Daisy beamed back.

They completed the interview fairly quickly, now that Daisy had gotten her message across. Obviously she'd called Kari and Gage in together to see them in the same room, and to warn Kari off. Like Kari was interested in starting up something with an ex-boyfriend.

Small-town life, Kari thought grimly. How could she have forgotten the downside of everyone knowing everyone else?

Daisy continued to coo over Gage and he continued to ignore her advances. Despite being incredibly uncomfortable, Kari couldn't help wondering about the state of their real relationship and vowed to ask Gage the next time she felt brave. In the meantime, she would do her best to avoid Daisy.

People in big cities thought nothing happened in small towns, she thought as she finally made her escape. People in big cities were wrong.

"You spoil me, Mama," Gage said a few nights later as he cleared the table at his mother's house.

Edie Reynolds, an attractive, dark-haired woman in her late fifties, smiled. "I'm not sure cooking dinner for you once a week constitutes spoiling, Gage. Besides, I need to be sure you're getting a balanced meal at least once in a while."

He began scraping plates and loading the dishwasher. "I'm a little too old to be eating pizza every night," he teased. "Just last week I had a vegetable with my steak."

"Good for you."

He winked at her as he worked. His mother shook her head, then picked up her glass of wine. "I'm still very angry with you. What were you thinking when you burst in on those bank robbers?" She held up her free hand. "Don't bother telling me you weren't thinking. I've already figured that out."

"I was doing my job. Several citizens were in danger and I had to protect them."

She set her glass down, her mouth twisting. "I guess this means your father and I did too good a job teaching you about responsibility."

"You wouldn't have it any other way."

"Probably not," she admitted.

The phone rang. His mother sighed. "Betty Sue from the hospital auxiliary has been calling me every twenty minutes about our fund-raiser. I'm amazed we got through dinner without her interrupting. This will just take a second." She picked up the receiver on the counter and spoke in a cheerful tone.

"Hello? Why, Betty Sue, what a surprise. No, no, we'd just finished eating. Uh-huh. Sure."

Edie headed for the living room. "If you want to rearrange the placement of the booths, you're going to have to clear it with the committee. I know they told you to run things, but..."

Gage grinned as he tuned out the conversation. His mother's charity work was as much a part of her as her White Diamonds perfume.

He finished with the dishes and rinsed the dishcloth

before wiping down the counters. Every now and then his mother protested that he didn't need to help after dinner, but he never listened. He figured she'd done more than her share of work while he and his brother Quinn were growing up. Loading the dishwasher hardly began to pay her back.

He finished with his chores and leaned against the counter, waiting for her to finish her conversation with Betty Sue. The kitchen had been remodeled about seven years ago, but the basic structure was still the same. The old house was crammed full of memories. Gage had lived here from the time he was born until he'd left to join the army.

Of course, every part of Possum Landing had memories. It was one of the things he liked about the town—he belonged here. He could trace his family back five generations on his father's side. There were dozens of old pictures in the main hallway—photos of Reynolds at the turn of the previous century, when Possum Landing had been just a brash, new cow town.

His mother returned to the kitchen and set the phone back on its base. "That woman is doing her best to make me insane. I can't tell you how sorry I am that I actually voted for her to run the fund-raiser. I must have been experiencing a black out or something."

He laughed. "You'll survive. How's the bathroom sink?"

"The leak is fixed. Don't fret, Gage. There aren't any chores for you this week."

She led the way back into the living room, where

they sat on opposite ends of the recovered sofa. Edie had replaced the ugly floral pattern with narrow-striped fabric.

"I don't invite you over just to get free labor," she said.

"I know, Mama, but I'm happy to help."

She nodded. "Will you be all right when John takes over that sort of chore?"

His mother had never been one to walk around a problem—if she saw trouble, she headed right for it. He leaned forward and lightly touched the back of her hand.

"I've told you before, I'm pleased about John. Daddy's been gone five years. You're getting a second chance to be happy."

She didn't look convinced.

"I'm telling the truth."

He was. The loss of his father had been a blow to both of them. Edie had spent the first year in a daze. Finally she'd pulled herself together and had tried to get on with her life. A part-time job she'd taken for something to do rather than because she needed the money had helped. As had her friends. Nearly a year before, she'd met John, a retired contractor.

Gage was willing to admit that he'd been a bit put off by the thought of his mother dating, but he'd quickly come around. John was a solid man who treated Edie as if she were a princess. Gage couldn't have picked better for his mother himself.

"You'll still come to dinner, won't you? Once we're married?"

"I promise."

He'd been coming to dinner once a week ever since he'd returned to Possum Landing after being in the army. Like many things in his life, it was a tradition.

His mother's dark gaze sharpened a little and he braced himself. Sure enough, she went right for the most interesting topic.

"I heard Kari Asbury is back in town."

"Subtle, Mama." He grinned. "According to Kari, she's not back, she's here for a short period of time while she fixes up her grandmother's house and sells it."

Edie frowned. "And then what? Is she going back to New York? She's a lovely girl, but isn't she getting a little old to be a fashion model?"

"She's going to be a teacher. She has her credentials and is applying for jobs in different parts of Texas."

"Not Possum Landing?"

"Not as far as I can tell."

"Are you all right with that?"

"Sure."

"If you're lying to me, I'm not averse to getting out the old switch."

He grinned. "You'd have to catch me first. I'm still a fast runner, Mama."

Her face softened with affection. "Just be careful, Gage. There was a time when she broke your heart. I would hate to see that happen again."

"It won't," he said confidently. A man was allowed to be a fool for a woman once in a lifetime, but not twice. "We'll always be friends. We have too much past between us to avoid that. We're neighbors, so I'll be seeing her, but it won't amount to anything significant.''

It was only a white lie, he thought cheerfully. Because getting Kari into bed was definitely his goal. And if things were as hot between them as he guessed they would be, the event would certainly qualify as "significant." But that wasn't something he wanted to share with his mother.

"You heard from Quinn lately?" he asked, changing the subject.

"Not since that one letter a month ago." She sighed. "I worry about that boy."

Gage didn't think there was any point in mentioning that Quinn was thirty and a trained military operative. "Boy" hadn't described him in years.

"He should be getting leave in the next few months."

"I'm hoping he'll make time to come to the wedding. I don't know if he will, though."

Gage wasn't sure, either. He and Quinn had once been close, but time and circumstances had changed things. They'd both headed into the military after high school, but unlike Gage, Quinn had stayed in. He'd gone into Special Forces, then joined a secret group that worked around the world wherever there was trouble.

Despite being from the same family as Gage, Quinn had never fit in. Mostly because their father had made his life a living hell.

As always, the thought made Gage uncomfortable. He'd never understood why he'd been the golden boy of the family and Quinn had been the unwelcome stranger. He also didn't know why he was thinking so much about the past lately.

Maybe it was Kari returning and stirring it up. Maybe now was a good time to ask a question that should have been asked long ago.

"Why didn't Daddy like Quinn?"

Edie stiffened slightly. "What are you saying, Gage? Your father loved you two boys equally. He was a good father."

Gage stared at her, wondering why she was lying. Why avoid the obvious?

"The old farmer's market opened last week. I'm going to head over there this weekend and see if I can get some berries. Maybe I'll bake a pie for next time."

The change of subject was both obvious and awkward. Gage hesitated a second before giving in and saying that he always enjoyed her pies.

But as they chatted about the summer heat and who was vacationing where, he couldn't shake the feeling that there were secrets hiding just below the surface. Had they always been there and he had never noticed?

Twenty minutes later, he hugged his mother goodbye, then picked up the trash bag from the kitchen and carried it out as he did every time he left. He put it in the large container by the garage and waved before stepping into his truck.

His mother waved back, then returned to the house.

Gage watched the closed back door for a while before starting the truck and heading home. What had happened tonight? Was something different, or was he making something out of nothing?

He slowly drove the familiar streets of Possum Landing. The signal by the railroad tracks had already started its slow flashing for the night. Those downtown would stay on until midnight, but on the outskirts of town they went to flashing at eight.

Unease settled at the base of his spine, making him want to turn around and demand answers from his mother. The problem was, he wasn't sure what the questions were supposed to be.

Maybe instead of answers, he needed a woman. It had been a long time and his need hadn't gone away. There were, he supposed, several women he could call on. They would invite him inside for dessert…and breakfast. He paused at the stop sign. No doubt Daisy would do the happy dance if he turned his attention in her direction. Of course, she would want a whole lot more than breakfast. Daisy was a woman in search of a happy ending. Gage was sure it was possible—just not with him.

He drummed his fingers on the steering wheel, then swore and headed home. None of those welcoming beds appealed to him tonight. They hadn't in a long time. He'd reached that place in his life where the idea of variety only made him tired. He wanted the familiar. He wanted to settle down, get married and have a half-dozen kids. So why couldn't he make it happen? Why hadn't he fallen in love and popped the question? Why hadn't he—

He turned into his driveway, his headlights sweeping the front of the house next door. Someone sat on the top step, shielding her eyes from the flash of light.

A familiar someone who made parts of him stand up at attention without even trying.

Been there, done that, he told himself as he killed the engine and stepped out into the quiet of the night. But that didn't stop him from heading toward her, crossing his lawn and then hers.

Anticipation filled him. He wondered how she liked her eggs.

Chapter Four

Kari watched as Gage approached. He moved with the liquid grace of a man comfortable in his own skin. He was what people called "a man's man," which made the most female part of her flutter. How ironic. She'd spent nearly eight years surrounded by some of the most handsome, appealing male models New York had to offer—a good percentage of whom had *not* been gay—and she'd never once felt herself melt just by watching them move. What was it about Gage that got to her? Was she just a sucker for a man in uniform, or was it something specific about him?

"So, how was your date?" she asked to distract herself from the liquid heat easing through her belly. "You're back early, so I'm going to guess the ever-delightful Daisy is playing hard to get."

She thought about mentioning her surprise that Daisy would let Gage leave without visiting the promised land, but was afraid the comment would come out sounding catty.

He settled next to her on the front step and rested his forearms on his knees. "You always were a nosy thing back when you were in high school. I see that hasn't changed."

"Not for a second." She grinned.

He glanced at her and gave her an answering smile that made her heart do a triple flip.

"I had dinner with my mother," he said. "I do it every week."

"Oh."

She tried to think of a witty comeback but couldn't. The admission didn't surprise her. Gage had always been good to the women in his life…his mother, her grandmother. She remembered reading an article somewhere, something about paying attention to how a man treats his mother because it's a good indication of how he'll treat his wife. Not that she was planning on marrying Gage Reynolds. Still, it was nice to reconfirm that he was one of the good guys.

"How *is* your mom?" she asked.

"Good. She had a rough time after my dad died. They'd been together for so long, I'm not sure she thought she could make it without him. Eventually she got it together. Last year she started dating again. She met a guy named John. They're engaged."

Kari straightened. "Wow. That's great." Then she remembered how close Gage had been to his father. "Are you okay with it?"

He nodded. "Sure. John is one of the good guys."

Takes one to know one, Kari thought. "When's the wedding?"

"This fall. He's a retired contractor. He has a lot of family up in Dallas. That's where he is this week. One of his granddaughters is having a birthday, and he wanted to be there for the party."

"They say people who have one successful marriage can have another."

Gage stared up at the night. "I believe that's true. My folks loved each other. There were plenty of fights and difficult times, but on the whole, they were in love. From what John has said about his late wife, they had a strong marriage, too. I figure the two of them are going to do just fine."

"I'd like to see your mother again. I always liked her."

"She's working up at the hardware store. It's a part-time job to get her out of the house. You should head on up and say hi."

"I will."

When Kari and Gage had been dating, Edie had welcomed her with open arms. Kari didn't know if the woman had done that with all Gage's girlfriends, but she liked to think she and Edie had been especially close. Of course, Edie wouldn't have been thrilled about her dumping Gage via a note and running away.

"Is she still mad at me for what I did?"

He glanced at her, laughter lurking in his dark eyes. "She seems to have recovered."

"Okay. Then, I'll pop over and congratulate her on

the upcoming nuptials. I think it's great that she's found someone. No one should be alone.''

As soon as the words fell from her mouth, she wanted to call them back. Obviously, both she and Gage were alone. She knew her circumstances—but what were his? He was the kind of man who had always attracted women, so the choice to be single must have been his. Why?

She was about to ask, when he beat her to the punch.

"So, why aren't you married, Kari?"

Before she could answer, he shrugged. "Never mind. I forgot. You weren't interested in home and hearth. You had things to do and places to be."

She bristled. "That's not true. Of course I want to get married and have kids. I've always wanted that."

"Just not with me?"

He didn't look at her as he spoke, and she didn't know what he was thinking.

"Just not on your timetable," she told him. She sighed. "Eight years ago, you were right on track with your life. You had seen the world and were ready to settle down. I was a senior in high school with a lot of unrealized dreams. I was young and hopeful, and as much as I cared about you, I was terrified by your life plan. You seemed so much older—so sure of yourself. Everything you said was reasonable, yet it felt wrong for me at the time. I didn't want to be like my mother and grandmother, marrying out of high school, having kids right away. I wanted *my* chance to see the world and live my dreams."

"I thought I was one of your dreams."

"You were. Just not right then. When I heard you were going to propose, I panicked, which is why I ran away. I thought…" She hesitated. "You were so clear on the way everything would be. I was afraid I'd get lost in that."

He sat close enough for her to feel the heat of his body and inhale the scent of him. She was torn between wanting to lean against him and heading for the hills. Confessions in the night were frequently dangerous. What would be the outcome of this one?

Gage surprised her by saying "You're right."

She blinked at him. "I didn't expect that."

He shrugged. "I thought I knew everything back then. You were what I wanted in a wife, we were in love—why wouldn't we get married and settle down? You talked about going to New York and being a model, but I didn't think you were serious." He glanced at her and shrugged again. "That was pretty arrogant of me. I'm sorry, Kari. I should have listened to you. Instead I focused on what I wanted and tried to steamroll my way to the finish line."

His confession caught her off guard. "Thanks," she murmured. "I wish we'd had this conversation eight years ago."

"Me, too. Maybe we would have found a way to make it work."

She nodded but didn't say anything. Privately, she doubted that would have happened. Even after all this time, the truth still hurt her. Gage might have wanted to marry her, but he hadn't loved her enough to come after her and ask her to return home with him. He hadn't loved her enough to get in touch with her and say he would wait while she followed her dreams. She took off, and he seemed to simply get on with his life.

"So I went into the army when I wanted to see the world and you went off to New York," he said lightly, as if trying to shift the tone of their conversation. "I'm guessing you had a better time."

She tamped her sadness and laughed. "Oh, I don't know. At least you got regular meals."

"Was money that tight?"

"A little. At first. But I got some part-time jobs and eventually modeling work. The food thing is more about being the American ideal of a working model. I didn't eat because I had to lose weight. I was young and determined, which meant I wasn't sensible. It wasn't a very healthy lifestyle."

"Aside from the lack of food, is it what you thought it would be?"

"I don't know. I think young women want to be models because it's glamorous. Where else can an eighteen-year-old girl make that kind of money and travel all over the world? There are lots of invitations. Men want to date models. Being a model is an instant identity."

She pulled her knees close to her chest and wrapped her arms around her legs. "But the reality can be difficult. Thousands of girls come to New York, and only a tiny percentage make it to supermodel status. A few more are successful. I was a little below that—a working model who earned enough to pay the bills and put myself through college, with a bit of a nest egg left over. The truth is, I never fit in.

I found some of the parties were scary places. I wasn't allowed to eat, I never was one to drink. And men who only date models have expectations I wasn't comfortable with.''

She smiled at him. ''I guess you can take the girl out of Possum Landing, but you can't take Possum Landing out of the girl.''

''I'm glad.''

As he studied her, she wondered what he was thinking. Had her experiences shocked him? Compared with most of her friends, she'd practically been a nun, but she wasn't going to tell Gage that. It would sound too much like making excuses.

''You were talking about finding a teaching job near Dallas,'' he said. ''Will you miss New York?''

''Some things, but I'm ready for a change. I was born and bred in Texas. This is where I belong.''

He rubbed the cracked paint on the handrail. ''What are your plans for the old house?''

Kari considered the question. ''I'm still debating.'' She suddenly remembered. ''Oh, I went around and did an inventory of furniture…mostly the antiques.''

Gage looked interested but didn't say anything.

She sighed. ''I loved my grandmother, but she was a bit of a pack rat. Anyway, I have a list. There are some I want to keep for myself…mostly those with sentimental value. I checked and my parents don't want anything. So I'm going to sell the others, except for the ones you'd like.''

He raised his eyebrows. ''What do you mean?''

''I didn't know if you were interested in antiques.

If you are, I'd like you to have first pick at what she had.''

"Why?"

Wasn't it obvious? "Come on, Gage, we both know how much you helped her. You were always willing to run over and fix whatever was broken. After I left, you kept her company and helped her out, even though you had to have been really angry with me."

''I wouldn't have let that affect my relationship with her.''

She noticed he didn't deny the anger, which made her uncomfortable. Funny how after all this time Gage's disapproval still had the power to make her cringe.

''That's my point,'' she said, staying on topic. ''You could have been difficult and you weren't. After she died, you contacted the real estate management company whenever there was a problem with the house. I owe you. I figured you'd be deeply insulted if I offered money, so this seemed like a good compromise.''

He stared at her. Despite the fact that the sun had gone down a while ago, the Texas summer night was still warm. As his intense gaze settled on her face, she had the feeling that the temperature had climbed a couple of degrees. Despite the fact that she was wearing shorts and a cotton sleeveless shirt, she felt confined…restricted…and far too *dressed*.

Kari couldn't help smiling. Boy, he was good. If he could make her writhe just by looking at her, what would happen if he ever kissed her again?

Too late, she remembered she'd promised herself she wasn't going to think of the kiss again. Not when she'd spent most of two days reliving it. She'd firmly put it out of her mind…almost.

"All right," he said slowly. "I'll consider taking one of the antiques as payment. If you haven't kept it for yourself, I wouldn't say no to the sideboard in the dining room."

It took her a second to figure out what on earth he was talking about. As far as her mind was concerned, the previous conversation hadn't even taken place. Then all her synapses clicked into place.

"No, I haven't claimed that one. Consider it yours."

"I'm much obliged."

His eyes held hers for a couple more heartbeats, then he finally looked away. She felt as if she'd been released from a force field. If she hadn't been sitting already, she would have collapsed.

She struggled to pick up the thread of their conversation. Oh, yeah. They'd been talking about her fixing up the house. "I'm going to paint the whole place," she said. "Inside and out. I'm doing the inside myself and hiring someone to do the outside."

Gage glanced up at the tall eaves and nodded. "Good idea. I'd hate to see you falling off a ladder."

"Me, too." She stretched out her legs in front of her. "There are a couple of windows that need replacing, and the whole kitchen is a 1950s disaster. I'll strip the cabinets and refinish them. I've already ordered new appliances and carpeting. I think that's about it."

"Sounds like you'll be busy."

"That's the plan. I'm going to start slow with the painting. Just do one room at a time. Everything needs a primer coat—it's been years between paint jobs."

He seemed to consider the night sky, then he turned to her. "I have a couple of days off coming up. I could offer you some brawn for moving things around and reaching the high places."

She shivered slightly at the thought of his "brawn." "I'm five-ten—I can reach the high places on my own. But I will say yes to whatever help you're willing to offer."

"Then, I'll be here."

She found herself leaning toward him as he spoke, as if what he said had great significance and she wanted to be close enough to breathe in every word. She sighed. Whatever was wrong with her was more serious than she'd thought. After all this time, she couldn't possibly still be crazy about Gage. Not when they'd both gone in such different directions.

He rose suddenly. "It's getting late," he said, moving off the stairs. "I should be getting back home."

She waited—more breathless than she wanted to admit—until he gave her a slight nod and headed toward his place.

"'Night, Gage," she called after him, as if his leaving was a good thing. As if she wasn't thinking about what it would be like if he kissed her again. Not that he was going to, obviously. Apparently, that one kiss had been enough for him. It had been enough for her, too. More than enough. In fact, she was really glad that he didn't plan to try anything. She would have to say no and it would get really embarrassing for both of them.

She *hated* that he hadn't kissed her.

By the next afternoon, Kari still hadn't figured out why. Why he hadn't and why it bugged her. Didn't Gage find her attractive? Hadn't he enjoyed their previous kiss? She *really* hated that his not kissing her had kept her up in the night nearly as much as his kissing her had.

It was the past, she told herself as she stood in her grandmother's bedroom and slowly opened dresser drawers. But after all this time, she was finding herself being sucked back into what had once been.

Kari shook her head to chase away the ghosts, then plopped on the floor to study the contents of the bottom drawer. There were several sweaters wrapped in lengths of cotton and protected by cedar chips. She held up a pale blue sweater, admiring the workmanship and the old-fashioned style. This particular sweater had been a favorite. Kari could see her grandmother in it as clearly as if the woman stood in front of her.

"Oh, Grammy, I miss you," she whispered into the silence of the morning. "I know you've been gone a long time, but I still think about you every day. And I love you."

Kari paused, then smiled slightly as she imagined her grandmother whispering back that she loved her favorite girl, too. More than ever. Despite everything, her grandmother had been the one constant in her life.

Kari slowly put the sweater back. She realized she needed a few boxes so she could sort those items that were going with her from those that were not. She touched the sweater before closing the drawer. That she would keep. It would be a talisman—her way to connect to some of her happiest memories.

The middle drawer yielded scarves and gloves, while the top drawer held her grandmother's costume jewelry. There were plenty of real pieces, Kari remembered as she touched a pin in the shape of a dragonfly. They were in a jewelry chest on the top of the dresser. A string of pearls and matching earrings, a few gold chains. Perhaps her grandmother had worn them, too, but all of Kari's memories of the woman who had raised her were much more connected with the costume pieces.

There were the gaudy necklaces that Kari had dressed up in when she was little and the fake pearl choker her grandmother had worn to church every Sunday. The bangle bracelets and the butterfly earrings and the tiny enameled rose pin Kari had been allowed to wear on her first date with Gage.

She shifted on the floor so that she leaned against the old bed. The rose pin didn't look the worse for wear. She rubbed her fingers across the smooth petals, remembering how her grandmother had pinned it on Kari's blouse five minutes before Gage had arrived to pick her up.

"For luck," her grandmother had said with a smile.

Kari smiled, too, now, even as she fought tears. Back then she'd wanted every bit of luck available. She hadn't been able to believe that someone as grown up and handsome as Gage Reynolds had asked her out. When he'd issued the invitation, it had been all she could do not to ask him why he'd bothered.

But she hadn't. And when she'd gotten nervous on that date, she'd touched the rose pin for luck. It had happened so many times, Gage had finally commented on the tiny piece of jewelry.

They'd been walking out back, Kari remembered, her mouth trembling slightly as she battled with tears. After a dinner at which she'd barely managed to swallow two bites, he'd taken her for a walk in the pecan grove.

She could still smell the earth and hear the crunch of the fallen pecans under their feet. She'd thought then that he might kiss her, but he hadn't. Instead, he'd taken her hand in his. She'd almost died right there on the spot.

It wasn't that no one had held her hand before. Other boys had. But that was the difference…they were boys. Gage was a man. Still, despite the age difference and her complete lack of subtlety, he'd laced his fingers with hers as they'd walked along. Kari had relived the moment for days.

They'd been out exactly five times before he finally kissed her. She touched the pin again, smiling as she remembered pinning it on her sweater that October evening. Once again, Gage had taken her to dinner and she'd only managed to eat a third of her entrée. She hadn't been dieting—that didn't come until her move to New York. Instead, she'd been too nervous to eat. Too worried about putting a foot wrong or appearing immature. After only five dates, she was well on her way to being in love with Gage. Her fate had been sealed that evening, as she leaned against the pecan tree, her heart beating so fast it practically took flight.

She closed her eyes, still able to feel the tree pressing into her back. She'd been scared and hopeful and apprehensive and excited, all at the same time. Gage had been talking and talking and she'd been wishing he would just *do it*. But what if he didn't want to kiss her? What if…

And then he had. He'd lightly touched the pin, telling her how pretty it was. But not as pretty as her. Then, while she was still swooning over the compliment, he'd bent low and brushed his mouth to hers.

Kari sighed softly. As first-kiss memories went, she would bet that hers was one of the best. Before then, she'd dated some, and kissed some, but never anyone like him. In fact, she couldn't remember any of her first kisses with other boys. But she remembered Gage. Everything from the way he'd put his hand on her shoulder to how he'd stroked her cheek with his warm fingers.

A shiver caught her unaware as it lazily drifted down her back. The restless feeling returned, and with it all the questions as to why he hadn't bothered to kiss her again the previous night.

Impulsively, she fastened the rose pin to her T-shirt. Maybe she was still floundering around in her love life, but she had some fabulous memories. However it might have ended, Gage had treated her incredibly well when they were together. There weren't many men like him.

She had the brief thought that it would be wonderful to be meeting him now, for the first time. She had a feeling that without all their past baggage to trip over, they could make something wonderful happen between them.

The daydream sustained her for a second or two, until she reminded herself that it didn't matter what would or would not be happening if she and Gage had just met. Possum Landing was his world, and she was most definitely not back to stay.

Chapter Five

After walking through the upstairs and deciding on paint colors, Kari made a list and headed for the hardware store. Since she'd last been in Possum Landing, one of those new home improvement superstores had opened up on the main highway about ten miles away. She was sure their selection was bigger, their prices were lower and that she probably wouldn't run into one person she knew. But starting a refurbishing project without stopping by Greene's Hardware Center would probably cause someone from the city council to stop by with a written complaint. Her grandmother had always taught her the importance of supporting the local community. And old Ed Greene had owned the store since before Kari was born.

New York was a big city made up of small neighborhoods. Over time, Kari had come to know the people who worked at the Chinese place where she ate once a week, and she and the lady at the dry cleaner had been on speaking terms. But those relationships hadn't had the same history that existed here in Possum Landing.

So she drove across town to Greene's, then pulled into the parking lot that had last been repaved in the 1980s. The metal sign was still there, as was an old advertisement for a certain brand of exterior paint. Advertising slogans, long out of date, covered most of the front windows.

Kari smiled in anticipation, knowing there would be a jumble of merchandise inside. If she wasn't careful she would come out with more than just paint. She still remembered the old rooster weather vane her grandmother had come home with one afternoon. For the life of her, she couldn't figure out how Ed had talked her into buying it.

Kari pulled her list out of her purse, determined to be strong. She walked up the creaking steps of the building's front porch and stepped into the past.

Old file cabinets stood by the front door. They contained everything from stencils to paint chips, instruction on lawn care and packets of exotic grass seeds. To the right was a long wooden counter with Peg-Board behind it. Dozens of small tools hung in a seemingly unorganized array. The place smelled of dust and cut wood and varnish. For a moment Kari felt as if she were eight again. She could almost hear her grandmother calling for her to stay out of trouble.

"Kari?"

The female voice was familiar. Kari turned and saw Edie Reynolds walking in from the back room. Gage's mother was a tall, dark-haired woman, still attractive and vibrant. She smiled broadly as she approached and pulled Kari into a welcoming hug.

"I'd heard you were back in town," Edie said when she released her. "How are you? You look great."

"You, too," Kari managed to say, too surprised by the friendly greeting to protest that she wasn't back for any length of time. She knew that Gage's mother would have known about her son's plans to propose and that she, Kari, had broken off the relationship in a less than honorable way. Apparently, Edie had decided to forgive and forget.

Edie pulled out one of the stools in front of the counter and took a seat, then motioned for Kari to do the same.

"Tell me everything," the older woman said. "You're staying at your grandmother's house, right?" She smiled. "Actually, I suppose it's your house now."

"I still think of it as hers," Kari admitted. "I want to fix it up and sell it. That's why I'm here. I need supplies."

"We have plenty." Edie laughed. "So you were in New York. Did you like it? Gage showed me some of your pictures. You were in some pretty big magazines."

"I managed to make a living. But it wasn't the career I thought I wanted. I went to college and just received my teaching credentials."

"Good for you." Edie glanced around the store. "As you can see, nothing's changed."

Kari didn't know if she agreed or not. Some things seemed different, while others—like her reaction to Gage—didn't seem to have evolved at all.

"You working here is different," Kari said. "I only remember seeing Ed behind the counter."

"That old coot," Edie said affectionately. "I took a part-time job a year or so after Ralph died. I didn't need the money, but I desperately needed to get out of the house. The walls were starting to close in on me."

"I'm sorry about Ralph," Kari said.

Edie sighed. "He was a good man. One of the best. I still miss him, of course. I'll always miss him." She smiled again. "Which probably makes the news of my engagement a little hard to understand."

"Not at all. I think it's wonderful you found someone."

"We met right here," Edie said, her eyes twinkling. "He's retired now, but he was still working then. A contractor on a job. He ran out of nails and popped in to buy some. It was just one of those things. I had started dating a few months before and really hated the whole process, but with John... everything felt right. Somehow I knew."

Kari envied Edie her certainty. She'd dated from time to time, and no man had ever felt right. Well, Gage had, but that had been years ago.

"When's the wedding?" Kari asked.

"This fall. We're still planning the honeymoon. I can't wait."

"It sounds wonderful."

"I'm hoping it will be. Now, enough about me, tell me about yourself. I'll bet you never expected a bank robbery to welcome you back."

Kari nodded. "I managed to avoid crime the whole time I was in New York, but after less than twenty-four hours in Possum Landing I had a man holding a gun to my head." She touched Edie's arm. "Gage was very brave."

"I know. I hate that he put himself in danger, but as he pointed out to me, it's his job. I tell myself that the good news is he doesn't have to do it very often. Possum Landing is hardly a center of criminal activity."

They chatted for a few more minutes, then Edie helped Kari buy primer and paint, brushes, rollers, tarps and all the other supplies she would need for her painting project.

She left the hardware store with her trunk full and her spirits light. There was something to be said for a place where everyone knew her name.

"You'd better be awake or there's going to be hell to pay," Gage called as he strolled in through the back door without knocking.

Kari didn't bother looking up at him. Instead, she grabbed another mug from the cupboard and filled it with hot coffee.

"Good morning to you, too," she said, turning to face him as she handed him the mug.

Whatever else she'd started to say fled her brain as she took in the worn jeans and tattered T-shirt he wore. She'd only seen him in his uniform since she'd returned to Possum Landing, and while the khaki shirt and pants emphasized the strength of his body, they had nothing on worn denim.

What was it about a sexy man in blue jeans? Kari wondered as her chest tightened slightly. Was it the movement of strong thigh muscles under fabric made soft by dozens of washings? The slight fading by the crotch, or the low-slung settling on narrow hips? She barely noticed the cooler he set on her kitchen table.

"I have a list of demands," he said after taking a sip.

She blinked. "Demands for what?"

"Work. I might work for free, but I don't come cheap. I expect a break every two hours and I expect to be well fed. Before we start, I want to know what's for breakfast and lunch."

She burst out laughing, but Gage didn't even crack a smile.

"Okay, big guy," she said. "Here's the deal. Take a break whenever you want—I don't care how often or how long. Seeing as I'm not paying you, I can't really complain. There's cold cereal for breakfast and I have sandwich fixings for lunch. Oh, and you'll be making your own sandwich."

Gage muttered something about Kari not being a Southern flower of motherhood, then started opening cupboards. "Cereal," he complained. "Aren't you even going to offer me pancakes?"

"Nope."

He muttered some more. "I'm just glad I stopped by my mama's place. She made potato salad and macaroni salad. I'll share, but that means you have to make my sandwich.''

"Blackmail."

"Whatever works."

She poured herself more coffee and sighed. "All right. It's a deal."

He poked through her cereal collection, which consisted of several single-serving boxes.

"You turned into a Yankee while you were gone. I'll bet you can't even make grits anymore."

"I couldn't make them when I lived here, so you're right. I can't make them now."

He pretended outrage. "I could arrest you for that, you know. This is Possum Landing. We have standards."

She topped off his coffee mug, then started for the stairs. "If you're done complaining, let's get to work."

"Oh, great. No pancakes, you won't make my sandwich and now you're turning into a slave driver. Don't that just beat all?"

Kari chuckled as she reached the second floor. Gage's teasing had managed to divert her attention from his jeans and what they did to her imagination…not to mention her libido. Far better to play word games than dream about other kinds of games. That would only get her into trouble.

"I thought we'd start in here," she said, walking into one of the small spare bedrooms. "I haven't painted in years and I doubt I did a very good job when I was twelve. So I'm trying to gear up."

He looked around. She'd taken out the smaller

pieces of furniture and had pushed the rest into the center of the room.

After setting his mug on a windowsill, Gage grabbed a four-drawer dresser and picked it up. "Let's get rid of a little more so we have room to work," he said. "Where can I put this?"

She stared at him. Last night she'd practically pulled a muscle just trying to move the dresser across the floor. Gage picked it up as if it weighed as much as a cat. Figures.

"In my grandmother's room."

He followed her down the hall. "Are you sleeping in there? Isn't it the biggest bedroom?"

"No and yes. I'm in my old room. I just felt better being in there."

He put down the dresser and turned. "She wouldn't mind," he said seriously. "She loved you."

"I know. I just…" How to explain? "I want to keep the memories as they are."

"Okay."

He put his arm around her as they walked back to the spare room. Kari tried not to react. Gage's gesture was friendly, nothing more. Nothing romantic…or sexual. Her imagination was working overtime and she was going to make it stop right this minute.

So why did she feel each of his fingertips where they touched her bare arm? And why did the hairs on the back of her neck suddenly stand at attention?

"I, uh, did some patching yesterday," she said, slipping free of his embrace. Casual or not, his touch made her breathing ragged. "There were some nail holes and a few cracks. I guess we sand it next."

He stepped around her and studied her supplies. "I'll sand. It's man's work."

"*Man's* work?"

"Sure."

"What will I be doing while you're dragging home the woolly mammoth?"

"You can clean up your putty knife and take off the baseboards."

She eyed the strips of wood encircling the room just above the carpeting. "Why isn't that man's work?"

He sighed. "If I have to explain everything, we'll never get the painting started, let alone finished."

"Uh-huh. Why do I know this is more about you doing what you want to do than defining tasks by gender?"

Gage looked up blankly. "I'm sorry. Did you say something?"

Kari thought about throwing something at him, but laughed, instead. While he went to work with sandpaper, she knelt on the opposite side of the room and gently began to pull the baseboards free of the wall.

They worked in silence for nearly half an hour.

"You do good work," Gage said finally.

"Thanks. I can read directions. Plus, I've learned to be good at odd jobs."

"Why is that?"

"The need to eat and pay rent," she said easily. "I told you, I didn't get any modeling work for over a year. New York isn't exactly cheap. So I worked different places to support myself. Some months it was tough."

He finished sanding and picked up a screwdriver. In a matter of seconds, he'd popped the pins out of the hinges and removed the door.

"You didn't call home and ask for money."

It was a statement, not a question. Obviously, he and Grammy had talked about her after she'd left.

"Nope. It had been my decision to leave, so it was my responsibility to make it on my own. I didn't want to get complacent, thinking that I always had someone waiting to send me money. The only thing I allowed myself was the promise my grandmother had made to send me a ticket home should I ever want it."

"Were you tempted?"

"A couple of times. But I held on and then things began to turn around. I got my first well-paying modeling job right before she died. She didn't get to see the magazine spread, but she knew about it, so that was something."

Kari pulled off the last piece of baseboard and dragged it out into the hallway.

Gage reached for the can of primer. "You know she was proud of you," he said.

She nodded. "I know. She never made me feel bad for leaving, and she always said I was going to make it."

"And you did."

"Sort of. But in the meantime, there were all those other lovely jobs."

He poured primer into two small buckets, then took a brush and handed her another. "Any painting?" he asked.

"No. I think there's a union. I did more conventional things. Worked in retail, walked dogs, delivered packages."

"Waited on tables?"

She shook her head. "I didn't eat much, and being around food was torture. I tried to avoid restaurants whenever possible. My favorite gig was house-sitting. I stayed in some amazing places. Great views, soft beds, and not a cockroach in sight."

"Were you ever scared?" Gage asked.

"Sometimes. At first. I'd never been on my own. It was a trial by fire."

While Gage enjoyed hearing about her previous life, he didn't ask the one question he wanted to. Had she missed him? Had she thought about him after she left, or had she shaken off his memory like so much unwanted dust?

"It was quiet after you left," he said instead as he brushed primer on the wall by the window.

Kari crouched by the door frame. She half turned and glanced at him over her shoulder. "I'm sorry if…" Her voice trailed off. "I never asked because I was afraid of what I'd hear. I'm sorry if it was bad for you after…"

He knew what she meant. After she left. After she stood him up and walked out of his life. Word spreads fast in a small town and by prom night nearly everyone knew that he'd bought an engagement ring for Kari. It was months before well-meaning folk stopped asking "No, how are you *really?*"

"It wasn't so bad," he said, because it was true. The blow to his pride was nothing compared with the pain in his heart. He'd never been in love before. Having Kari walk away so easily had taught him a hard lesson—that being in love didn't guarantee being loved in return.

Until Kari had left him, he'd assumed they would spend the rest of their lives together. He'd planned a future that had included only one woman. Finding out she didn't share his dreams...or want to marry him...had shattered his hopes and broken his heart.

"I used to look for your pictures in women's magazines," he admitted.

She stood up and laughed. "I can't believe you bought them."

"Some. I went to the next town, though."

"I should hope so. We can't have one of Possum Landing's finest checking out fashion magazines." Her laughter faded. "I'm guessing you gave up long before you found me on one of the pages."

"Nope. I told you I saw that hair ad."

There had been others. It was nearly five years before he'd been able to let Kari go.

"That was my first big break," she said.

"I liked the lingerie spread," he teased. "You looked good in the black stuff, but the teal was my favorite."

The brush fell out of Kari's hand. Fortunately it tumbled onto the tarp rather than the carpet. She blinked at him as a flush climbed up her cheeks.

"You saw that?" she asked in a strangled voice.

"Uh-huh."

She cleared her throat, then realized she'd dropped her brush and picked it up. "Yes, well, I don't know how the regular lingerie models stand it. I hated wearing so little and how everyone stared at me. Plus, I was starving. I hadn't eaten for three days beforehand so I wouldn't be bloated. I started to get light-headed, so I worried that I was going to have a really spacey expression on my face and the client wouldn't like it.'' She shivered slightly. ''I never looked at those pictures when they came out. They were a part of my portfolio, but I avoided them.''

''You were beautiful,'' he said sincerely. ''I had no idea what was under all those clothes you used to wear.''

''Just the usual body parts.''

''It's all in the details, darlin'.''

Kari laughed.

They worked in silence for a few minutes. Gage didn't mind that they weren't talking. Being around Kari took some getting used to. At one time she'd been everything, then she'd been gone and he'd had to figure out how to make her not matter. Having her back confused him. While his body was very clear on what it wanted from her, the rest of him wasn't so sure.

Not that it was going to be an issue. She was moving on. Which meant anything other than sex would make him a fool for love twice. No way was he going to let that happen.

''I always wanted to thank you,'' Kari said as she poured primer into roller trays.

He noticed she was careful not to look at him.

''For what you did…or didn't do, when we were going out.''

He had no idea what she was talking about. "What didn't I do?"

She shrugged. "You know."

"Actually, I don't."

She turned to him. "You never pushed me. Now the age difference between us is nothing, but back then it was a big deal. You had been in the military and traveled the world. You'd seen and done things and you never…" Her voice trailed off.

Gage stared at her. "Are you talking about sex?"

For the second time in a half hour, she blushed. "Yes. You never pushed me. I didn't think it was a big deal back then, but now, I know that it was. You wanted things from me, but you never made me feel that I had to give in to keep you."

"You didn't. Kari, I wanted to marry you. I wasn't going to dump you because you were young and innocent."

"I know. I just want to thank you for that."

He wondered what kind of guys she'd met that would make her think his behavior was anything but normal.

She picked up a roller. "I thought you were a knight in shining armor that first night we met."

He frowned. "I was doing my job and you were damn lucky I came along."

"I know." She smiled sadly. "I was so excited to be invited to that party with real college boys. I'd never been to one before. One of my friends, Sally, had beer at her seventeenth birthday party, but that was a girls-only sleepover, and while it was exciting for us, it didn't have the same thrill as a boy–girl party with hard liquor.''

He shook his head. ''Unless you've changed, you're not much of a drinker at all.''

She laughed. ''Oh, I didn't want to drink any, I just wanted to be in with the cool kids. I never was all that popular.''

That surprised Gage. He remembered her having lots of friends in high school. But he knew that she'd never belonged to any one social group. Part of the reason was that Kari hadn't fit any label, part of it was that she had been so pretty. She'd intimidated the boys and alienated the girls.

''I was so scared,'' she said with a sigh. ''Walking down that back road by myself.''

''You should have been scared.''

He remembered their first official meeting. He'd moved back to Possum Landing after getting out of the service and had taken a job as a deputy. He'd bought his house a year later, right beside Kari's grandmother's place. While in the process of moving in, he'd noticed the pretty young woman next door. He hadn't thought anything of her at the time. Not until he'd been called out to a loud party on the edge of town.

Gage had given a warning and had known he would be called back in less than an hour. The second time he would get tough, but he always figured everyone deserved one chance to screw up. On his way back to the station he'd seen an old Caddy crawling along at about five miles an hour. The top was down and there were four very drunk college guys in the vehicle. Gage had hit his lights. A flash of movement on the side of the road had caught his attention. It was only then that he saw a teenage girl looking scared and out of place.

He'd sized up the situation in less than a minute. Girl goes to wild party, tries to escape and has no ride home, so she walks. Drunk boys follow, looking for trouble. He told her to climb into his squad car before telling the guys to walk back to the party or risk being arrested for drunk driving. They'd protested, but finally agreed. Gage had taken the keys, saying they could get them back the following day…as long as they were accompanied by a parent. Then he'd returned to his car to find a trembling teenager fighting tears.

He'd prayed she wouldn't break down before he got her home. It was only when she whispered her address that he realized she was his neighbor.

Now, all these years later, he remembered how concerned he'd felt. Kari was only a kid. But kid or not, she'd been drinking.

"You nearly threw up in my car," he complained, speaking his thoughts out loud.

Kari glared at him. "I did not. I got out of the car before I threw up."

"You looked awful."

"Gee, thanks. I felt awful. But you were really nice. You gave me your handkerchief afterward."

"You notice I didn't ask for it back."

She laughed. "Yes, I did notice that." She rolled on more primer. "I haven't thought about that night for a long time. I was in over my head. Everyone at the party was drunk. I drank some, but not enough to forget myself. Some of the boys wanted to have sex and I didn't.''

"So you started walking home."

"And you saved me."

"I gave you a ride."

"Yes, and then you lectured me on being stupid."

Gage remembered that. He hadn't let her out of the car until he'd given her a stern talking to. Her blue eyes had widened as he talked about the dangers of parties that could get out of hand.

He'd given the lecture several times before, but never had he been distracted by a passenger. He found himself having thoughts that didn't go with the job.

"Then you asked me how old I was," Kari continued. "I couldn't figure out why. I thought maybe it had something to do with arresting me."

"Not exactly."

"I know that, now."

"You'd been eighteen for two days," he said in disgust. "I was twenty-three, almost twenty-four. Six years seemed like a big gap back then."

"But you asked me out, anyway."

"I couldn't help myself."

He was telling the truth. Gage had tried to talk himself out of his attraction for nearly a month. Finally he'd gone to Kari's grandmother and sought her opinion.

"Grammy said it was fine," Kari said softly. "I think she really hoped I would marry you and live next door.''

She turned away suddenly, but not before Gage thought he saw tears in her eyes.

"She would have liked that," he said quietly, "but more than anything, she wanted your happiness."

"I know," she said with a nod. "It's just..." She glanced around the room. "Being back here makes me miss her. Silly, huh?"

"No. You loved her. That's never silly."

She gave him a grateful smile. He felt a tightening low in his gut. Being back might make her miss her grandmother, but it made Gage miss other things. Oddly enough, they were things that had never happened. He didn't have memories of making love with Kari, yet he knew exactly what the experience would be. He knew the taste of her and how she would feel. He knew the sounds she would make and the magic that would flare between them. Despite the years and the miles, he still wanted her.

"You always understand," she said.

"Not even close."

"You understood me before and you still understand me."

"Maybe you're just simple."

She chuckled. "That must be it."

He didn't want it to be anything else—he didn't want to have any kind of connection to Kari Asbury. Sex was easy, but anything else would be complicated...and potentially dangerous.

"You're probably just really good with women," she said. "I mean, I was gone on you in thirty seconds, and now Daisy obviously has the hots for you."

"I don't want to talk about either of you."

"You want to talk about me," she teased. "Don't you? Don't you want to take a long walk down memory lane?"

"Isn't that what we've been doing?"

"I guess." She stared at him. "Have you slept with her?"

He stared back. "No."

"You didn't sleep with me, either. You do have sex with some of them, don't you, Gage?"

He saw the twinkle in her eyes. He kept his face sober as he continued to paint. "Sure. But I'm sort of a go-all-night kind of lover and that cuts into my sleep. I can't take on any new women until I get rested again."

She groaned. "Oh, please."

"Right now? You want to do it on the tarp?"

She laughed, then her humor faded. "I'm sorry *you* weren't my first time," she said, not looking at him, then shrugged. "You probably didn't want to know that."

He was stunned by the confession, probably because he had so many regrets about the same thing. "I wanted that, too," he admitted. "I'd thought about it a lot, but I wanted to wait…"

"And then I was gone," she said, finishing the sentence. "I'm sorry. For a lot of things."

"Me, too."

They didn't speak for a while, but he didn't mind the silence. He'd always felt comfortable around Kari. He hadn't thought they needed to make peace with the past, but a little closure never hurt anyone.

Finally he put down his brush and stretched. "Hey,

I've been working way longer than two hours. It's time for a break. I think you should make my sandwich now.''

"Excuse me, I believe I told you I wasn't making anything. That you were on your own.''

She straightened, and he wrapped an arm around her shoulders. "Naw. You *want* to wait on me. It's a chick thing.''

"I'm tall and wiry, Gage. I could take you right now.''

He grinned. "Not even on a bet, kid.''

Chapter Six

"What do you mean you're not going to help me clean up?" Kari asked in pretended outrage after they'd finished lunch.

Gage leaned back in his chair, looking full and satisfied and very sexy.

"I made my own sandwich," he said, ticking off items on his fingers. "Despite protests. I brought the potato and macaroni salads."

"But you didn't make them. Your mom did."

"I carried them, and it's damn far from my house to yours." He held up another finger. "I'm providing free labor and charming company, so it seems to me that cleaning would clearly be your responsibility."

She shook her head, more charmed than irritated. "You need to get married so some woman can whip you into shape."

He glanced down at his midsection. "Don't you like my shape? I've never had complaints before."

She didn't want to think about how he looked in his worn jeans and T-shirt. Just a quick glance at his muscles and the way he moved was enough to make her squirm. Not that she was going to admit it.

"You're passable," she said, going for a bored tone.

"You're just used to those sissy boys in New York."

She laughed. "Some of them are pretty nice looking."

"Real men are born in Texas."

"Like you?"

He leaned toward her. "Exactly like me."

They were flirting, she realized. It wasn't something she did very often, mostly because she was afraid of messing up. But with Gage that didn't seem to matter. If she put a step wrong, he wouldn't say anything to make her feel bad. He was, as he had always been, safe.

The thought surprised her. Why would she still think of Gage as safe? What did she know about him? He could have changed. He probably had, she thought, but not in any ways that affected his character.

"Maybe I'll take a nap," he said.

She glared at him. "You will not. I'm practically paying you to help me, so you'll get your butt back upstairs and keep working."

He grinned. "Make me."

Something hot and sensual flared to life inside her.

Something that made her wish for a witty comeback or the physical courage to walk over there and—

The phone rang.

"Talk about being saved by the bell," Kari muttered as she crossed the kitchen.

"I'll go start work," he said, rising. "But don't you take too long. I'm keeping track of hours, and if I work more than you, there will be hell to pay."

She dismissed him with a wave and reached for the phone. "Hello?"

"Hello, darling. How are you doing?"

Her humor faded as if it had never been. Tension instantly filled her. "Hi, Mom. I'm great. What's up with you?" Kari hoped her mother didn't hear the tension in her voice.

"Your father and I are planning a trip soon. You know, the usual."

Kari did know. She hated the fact that twenty-plus years after the fact, the information still had the power to make her feel angry and bitter.

"I received your letter," Aurora Asbury continued. "I never understand why you write instead of calling. Although, I always enjoy hearing from you."

"Thanks," Kari said. She wasn't about to admit that she wrote because it was one-way communication and a whole lot easier than picking up the phone.

"How's the house?" Aurora asked. "It's so old. Are you really going to be able to fix it up?"

"Sure. It won't be too much work, and I'll enjoy the challenge." Kari pressed her lips together. She felt both startled to hear from her mother and guilty about the house. Her grandmother, Aurora's mother, had left it to her, not her mother. Of course, her mother had never been around. She and Kari's father had been traveling the world.

"I think your plan to sell it is a good one," her mother said. "I *had* thought you might want to keep it for old time's sake."

"I don't want to do that." Kari drew in a breath. "So, um, how's Houston?"

"Hot and humid." Aurora sighed. "I can't wait for your father's next assignment. We should be heading overseas soon. I'm hoping for something in the Far East, but you know the company. We never know for sure until he gets his assignment."

There was a pause and then, "Are you sure you'll be all right there in Possum Landing, darling? It's such a small, stifling town. You could always hire someone to update the house, and stay with us for a few weeks."

Kari felt a surge of irritation. The invitation was coming a few years too late. "I'll be fine here," she said. "I'm enjoying reminiscing."

"I don't understand why you would want to stay in Texas after living in New York, but it's your choice." She paused, then said, "I was thinking of coming up for a quick visit in the next few weeks."

Kari stiffened. "Sure. That would be great." What she really wanted to ask was "why?" but she didn't. Aurora had many faults, but since being cruel wasn't one of them, Kari refused to be cruel herself.

"I'm not sure. I'll let you know."

"Okay. Well, I need to get back to work. I'm starting the painting."

"All right, darling. You take care of yourself."

"You, too, Mom."

Kari said goodbye, then hung up. She stood in the kitchen for several minutes, trying to recapture her good mood. When it didn't happen, she figured Gage was the best antidote for a burst emotional bubble and headed up the stairs.

"You're late," he complained, the second she walked into the room. "I'm going to have to—" He broke off and stared at her. "What happened? Bad news?"

"No. Just my mom calling."

"And?"

"And nothing. She might come to visit."

Gage didn't say anything. He clearly remembered that her relationship with Aurora had always been difficult.

She shrugged and moved toward the tray of primer he'd set up for her. "I know I should let it go."

"No one is saying you have to."

"I guess." She walked to the last bare wall. "It's just that I can't get past what she did. I mean, why have a kid if you're just going to abandon it?"

She hunched her shoulders, anticipating that he would defend Aurora's decision, but he didn't.

Kari was grateful. Sometimes she was okay with the past—mostly when she was happy in her life and her mother didn't call. But sometimes she felt the same sense of loss and confusion she had when she was young.

Her parents had married when her mother was barely eighteen. Her father was a petrochemical engineer working for a large oil company. Kari had come along sixteen months after the wedding, and four months later, her father had received his first overseas assignment. Somehow the decision was made to leave Kari with her grandmother. It was supposed to be a temporary arrangement—there had been some concern about taking such a small child so far away. But somehow, Aurora had never returned to claim her daughter.

"I spent my whole life waiting for her to come back for me," Kari said as she rolled primer on the wall. "Don't get me wrong. I loved being with Grammy and, after a while, it would have been weird to leave everything and go live with them. But even though I was happy, it hurt."

Gage lightly touched her arm. She smiled at him gratefully. "The thing is," she continued, "they always used the excuse that they didn't want to take a baby with them overseas. But my brothers were born there and never sent back here."

"It's their loss," he said gently.

She attempted a smile. "I tell myself that, from time to time. Sometimes I even believe it."

She tried to shake off the emotional edginess, along with the pain. Her life was great—she didn't need her family messing things up.

"I'm okay," she said. "Really. Those of us who weren't raised in the perfect family have to learn to adjust."

Gage grinned. "We weren't perfect."

"Sure you were. Parents who loved each other. A

home, a brother you actually got to know and spend time with. What more could you ask for?''

''I guess when you put it like that.'' He shrugged. ''It wasn't always good for Quinn, though. He and Dad never got along.''

Kari had never met Gage's younger brother. Quinn had left to join the military before Kari met Gage.

''What was the problem?'' Kari asked.

''I never knew. Quinn was a bit of a rebel, but the trouble started long before that. It's almost as if…'' His voice trailed off.

Kari didn't want to pry, so she changed the subject. ''What's he doing now?''

''Still in the service.''

''Really? Doing what?''

''I have no idea. He's in some special secret group. They travel around the world and take care of…things. Quinn eliminates people.''

Kari nearly dropped her roller. ''He kills them?''

Gage nodded.

''For a living?''

''Yeah.''

She couldn't imagine such a thing. Killing people for any reason was outside of her realm of imagination. She wanted to ask more questions, but had a feeling Gage didn't want to talk about it further.

''Okay, then,'' she said. ''I guess the fact that one of my brothers is an accountant and the other is a zoologist is really boring by comparison.''

''It sure is.''

She stuck her tongue out at him.

"Childish," he muttered. "I see you haven't changed at all."

"Of course I have. I'm even more charming than when I left."

"That wouldn't have taken much. Besides, I'm the charming one in this relationship."

He grinned as he spoke, and she couldn't help laughing.

"What is it with you?" she asked.

"I think it's something in the water," he said with mock seriousness. "After all, the Reynolds family has been in Possum Landing for five generations. That makes us very special."

"Do you ever wonder what made them stop here in the first place?"

"Good sense."

"Right. Because everyone in America wants to live in a place called Possum Landing."

"You bet."

She continued to paint the wall, while he put a coat of primer on the closet door. They didn't talk for a time. When they finished the room and started to leave, she touched his hand.

"Thanks," she said. "For coming over and making me laugh."

His dark eyes flared slightly. "I'm glad I can help. No matter what, Kari, we were always friends."

Friends. Was that what she wanted, too?

They spent the rest of the afternoon moving furniture out of the second small bedroom, patching the walls and waiting for the primer to dry. By three, they'd put on the first coat of paint.

"It's such a girl color," Gage teased as he rolled yellow paint over the walls.

Kari looked up from the door frame, where she was painting trim. "It is not. Pink is a girl color. Yellow is neutral. I wanted something bright and cheerful that would open up the room."

"What about a skylight?"

She turned away to hide her grin. "I'm ignoring you."

"Your loss. Are you doing all the bedrooms up here in yellow?"

"I haven't decided." There were a total of four on this floor. Hers, her grandmother's and the two they were working on. "I want to do Grammy's room next, which means moving her furniture into here."

"Are you giving it away?"

"I'd like to keep the dresser, but, yes, the rest of it will go." She hesitated, feeling faintly guilty. "I *want* to keep all of it...or even if I don't, I think I should."

"Why?"

"Because it was hers. Because of the memories."

"I doubt she'll mind if you only keep what you like. Her purpose in leaving you the house wasn't to make you unhappy."

"I guess."

Sometimes Gage annoyed her by being sensible, but sometimes he got it just right.

They worked well together, she thought as she moved to paint around the window. The banter made her laugh, the companionship lightened her spirits. Being around Gage made her happy.

She shook her head slightly. *Happy.* When was the last time she'd enjoyed that particular emotion? She'd been content, even pleased with the direction of her life. But happy?

"I'm done in here," he said a few minutes later. "I'm going out back to start cleaning up the brushes and rollers."

"Okay. I'll just be a little longer."

He grabbed the equipment and headed for the stairs. Kari finished painting and followed him. She went out the back door and around to the side of the house—a spray of cold water caught her full in the face.

She screamed. "What on earth—?"

But that's as much as she got out before another blast of freezing water hit her in the chest. She shrieked and jumped back to safety. Okay, she thought as she brushed off her face and arms, if that's how he wanted to play it.

She ran to the other side of the house. Sure enough, she found a coiled hose, which she unscrewed from the tap and dragged around to the back door tap. A few quick twists had it connected. She turned the water on full, then went on the attack.

Gage obviously thought she'd headed into the house, because he stood bent over, cleaning brushes in a bucket and chuckling to himself. She caught him square in the backside.

He jumped and growled, then turned on her. The battle was on.

Kari raced to the safety of the far side of the yard. Her hose stretched that far, but his didn't. While she was able to attack directly, he was forced to arc water toward her. She danced easily out of its reach.

"Big, bad sheriff can't catch me," she teased as she blasted him. "Big, bad sheriff is all wet."

"Dammit, Kari!" He muttered something, then disappeared around the side of the house. Seconds later he appeared without the hose. He walked toward the tap by the back door and turned it off, then put his hands on his wet hips and stared at her. He looked unamused.

She dropped the hose and took off toward the far end of the yard. It had been about nine years since she'd tried to take the fence, but she was willing to give it a try. The alternative was getting caught.

"Don't you dare!" she yelled as she ran, not sure what she was telling him not to do.

"I dare just fine," he said, sounding way too close.

But she was nearly there. Just a few more feet of grass and then she would be—

He caught her around the waist, pulling her hard against him and knocking most of the air out of her. She struggled, gasping and laughing the whole time, but it was pointless. Gage's arm was like a steel band. A very wet, steel band.

"Let go of me," she demanded.

"Not until I teach you a lesson."

"You and what army?"

"I can do it just fine myself, little girl."

"I'm not a little girl."

"No. You're an all grown-up Yankee."

"Who are you calling a Yankee?"

He carried her like a sack to the center of the lawn, then released her. She took off instantly—and didn't get more than one step before he grabbed her again. This time when he pulled her against him, they were facing each other.

Her hair dripped in her face, as did his. They were both breathing hard and very, very close.

"Troublemaker," he murmured, staring into her eyes.

His were dark and unreadable, but that was okay. While she couldn't tell what was going on in his brain, there was enough action in his body to keep her occupied. He seemed to be pressing against her in a way that made her think of games more adult than a water fight. The expression of his face had changed as well. His features tightened with something that looked very much like passion. Which was okay with her—sometime in the past three seconds she'd gone from shivering to being filled with anticipation.

"Maybe you need a little trouble in your life," she said softly.

"Maybe I do. Maybe you do, too."

She didn't have an answer for that, which was a good thing, because there wasn't any time to speak. His mouth settled on hers and all rational thought fled.

His lips were still damp from the water, but not the least bit cool. The arm around her waist tightened, pulling her even closer. They connected everywhere that was possible, with her hands touching his shoulders and his tongue brushing against her bottom lip.

She parted for him instantly, wanting, *needing* to taste him. The second he stroked the inside of her lower lip, shivers began low in her belly and radiated out in all directions. Her breasts swelled within the confines of her damp bra. Her thighs pressed together tightly. A light breeze cooled her wet skin, but parts of her were getting plenty hot.

He cupped her face as he deepened the kiss. She clung to him, wanting him to claim her, mark her, do with her whatever he wanted. She longed to be possessed by him.

Her fingers curled into his shoulders. Then she moved her hands to his back where she could feel the hard breadth of his muscles. His tongue circled hers, teasing, touching, seducing. She answered in kind, straining toward him. Every part of her melted against him.

Her breasts ached where they flattened against his hard chest. Her nipples tightened unbearably. When his hands moved to her waist, her breath caught.

His fingers moved higher and hers moved lower. While he inched his way up her damp T-shirt along her rib cage, she slipped down to his waist. Her heart thundered loud and fast until it was all she could hear. Her body trembled. Her thoughts circled, almost frenzied, unable to figure out what to concentrate on. The fabulous kiss? The slow ascent to her chest? The brush of damp jeans against her palms as she moved lower still?

He reached her breasts at the same instant she cupped his tight, high rear. Which was remarkable timing, because when his hands brushed against her, fire ripped through her body, making her gasp and nearly lose her balance. She grabbed on to him and squeezed, which caused him to arch against her. As his thumbs swept over her hypersensitive nipples, his hips bumped hers and she felt his need.

Pleasure shot through her. From their kiss, from the gentle stroking on her sensitive, aroused flesh, from the ridged maleness pressing into her belly. It was too much. It was amazing.

Gage pulled back just enough to put a little space between them. Before she could protest, he cupped her breasts fully, and she saw the wisdom in his actions. He explored her curves, brushing slightly, smoothing and inciting. Want filled her until she couldn't think about anything else...then he broke their kiss and began nibbling along her jaw and by her ear.

His hot breath tickled, his tongue teased, his teeth delighted. She clung to him as her world began to spin. There was only this moment, she thought hazily. The feel of Gage next to her, and what he did to her body.

She gasped when he nipped at her earlobe. Either he'd learned a whole lot while she'd been gone, or he'd been even more gentle back when they'd been going out because she didn't remember anything like this. Not ever. Back then, he'd kissed her and left her breathless, but he'd never—

She gasped as he walked behind her, licking her neck and sucking on her skin. He cupped her breasts at the same time and played with her nipples. Involuntarily, she opened her eyes and saw his large, strong hands moving against her. The combination of feeling and sight nearly made her collapse.

That was why the alarm bell caught her by surprise.

The alarm began as a distant, indistinct noise that grew louder with each beat of her heart, until it filled her head and made it impossible to concentrate on the delights Gage offered. It twisted her mind, clearing the sensual fog that surrounded her and forcing her to think sensibly.

What on earth was she doing? Did she really want to start something now? Like this? What would happen if she and Gage made love? Would it just be a quick trip down memory lane or would it be more? She hated that her brain insisted on being mature right now. Why couldn't she simply give in and then have recriminations later like everyone else?

Unfortunately the mood had been broken. She stepped away and sucked in a deep breath. It took more courage than she would have thought to turn and face him.

"I can't," she said, not quite looking him in the face. "I mean, I've never done the sex only thing. I'm not sure I could start now. So if anything were to happen—physically, I mean—it would lead to trouble. At least, for me."

She risked a glance and saw that he was looking at her with an intensity that made her take another step back. Not that she could read a single thought, which left her in the position of stumbling on with what she was trying to say.

"I'm leaving at the end of the summer. I would like us to be friends, but anything else…" She cleared her throat. "I just don't want to get my heart broken again. I mean, you already did that once."

Gage stared at Kari. He could accept that she wanted to call a temporary halt to their afternoon activities. Even he was willing to admit they'd gone a little too far, too fast. But that she had the guts to stand there and go on about *him* breaking *her* heart? His temper flared.

"What the hell are you talking about?" he demanded.

She blinked. "Excuse me?"

"I didn't break your heart. You're the one who left. You walked away without a backward glance. No warning, nothing. I was going to propose to you, Kari. I had planned to spend the rest of my life with you. You changed your mind and dumped me. So don't go telling me about *your* heart. You trampled mine pretty damn good."

Color rose to her cheeks. "That's not fair. I didn't deliberately set out to be mean. I wanted to talk to you but I couldn't. You didn't want to listen. You only wanted things your way, on your schedule."

He refused to be deflected from the point. "You dumped me without a word."

"I left a note."

He glared at her. "Yeah, a note. That's so great. I was about to propose and you left a lousy note. You're right. That makes everything fine."

"I'm not saying it makes things fine." She planted her hands on her hips. Her wet hair hung in her eyes; her mouth trembled as she spoke. "I couldn't risk speaking with you. I knew you'd do everything you could to change my mind. You would never understand why I had to leave.''

"I loved you. Of course I wouldn't want you to go away. Why is that so horrible?''

"It's not.'' She took a deep breath. "You're deliberately misunderstanding me. My point is, I deserved to have a life, too. I deserved to have my dreams and the opportunity to make them come true. But you didn't care about that. You weren't willing to listen. Besides, it's not as if you even missed me.''

Her words stunned him. He could still remember what it had been like when he found out she'd left. It was as if the world would never be right again.

"What the hell are you talking about? I was destroyed.''

"Right. And that's why you raced after me and begged me to come home. Admit it, Gage. You never really loved me. You loved the idea of getting married and starting a family. You certainly never cared enough to come after me and make sure I was all right.''

She ducked her head as she spoke, and for a second, he thought he saw tears in her eyes. He swore.

"Is that what this is about?'' he demanded. "Some stupid teenage girl test? If you really love me, you'll race after me to the ends of the earth?''

She raised her head. There *were* tears in her eyes, but he didn't care. He couldn't believe she was making him the bad guy in this.

"Yes, it was a test. And guess what? You failed.''

Fury overwhelmed him. He thought of all that had happened after she'd disappeared. How he'd raged and ached and thought he would never get over losing her. He thought about all the times he had gotten in his car to go after her, only to stop himself, because, dammit, letting her go had been the right thing to do. He thought about how he had looked for her in all those magazines, how he'd touched the glossy photo when he'd finally found her picture, still needing her as much as he needed to breathe.

He remembered that despite trying like hell to fall for someone else, he'd never been able to love anyone but Kari.

He thought about telling her all that—but why bother? She believed what she wanted to believe. So without saying anything, he turned on his heel and walked away.

Chapter Seven

"The nerve of that man" and other variations on the theme occupied all Kari's thoughts through the evening and well into the next day. She still couldn't believe what Gage had said to her. And how he'd acted! Like she'd said something so terrible.

Was it wrong of her to want to make decisions about her life? Of course not. But he'd refused to see that, just like he'd refused to understand what she'd been trying to say. Okay, maybe running away from a man she knew wanted to marry her, without explaining why and leaving only a note, wasn't very mature, but she'd been barely eighteen years old. Certainly not old enough to be getting engaged, let alone getting married and having kids! Which was what Gage had wanted. He'd planned it all out, from the

date of their wedding to how long they would wait
before starting a family to how many children were
going to make up that family.

She'd gotten scared. She'd panicked and run.

She flopped down on the sofa in the parlor and
stared out the front window. Upstairs there was plenty
of work to be done, but she couldn't seem to motivate
herself to do it.

Not only was she uncomfortable about arguing
with Gage, but she hated all the memories that fight
had stirred up. She'd been so in love with him, so
crazy for him, that leaving had been incredibly hard.
She'd cried the whole way to New York, and then
some. She'd wanted to return home, and a thousand
times she'd nearly done that. She'd picked up the
phone to call him twice that many times. But, in the
end, she hadn't. Because she'd known that coming
back to Possum Landing would mean giving in to
what Gage wanted for her life. It wasn't only the loss
of her dreams that she feared…it was the loss of herself.

But he hadn't seen it that way back then, or yesterday. They'd both said things they didn't mean—at
least, she hoped they didn't—and now they weren't
speaking.

Kari stirred restlessly on the sofa and frowned. She
didn't want to be *not* speaking to Gage. He was an
important part of her past and about her only real
friend in town. He was a good man and she really
liked him. Obviously, her body thought he was a de-
ity—but what did her body know? Avoiding each
other didn't make any sense.

That decided, she headed for the kitchen where a batch of peanut butter cookies were cooling. After transferring all but a half dozen onto a plate, she went upstairs and changed into a bright blue sleeveless dress and a pair of tan sandals. She fluffed her hair, touched up her lipstick and practiced her best smile.

She would make the first move to show good faith and get things right between them. Once they were speaking again, she would do her best to avoid conversations about the past, because that only seemed to get them in trouble. Oh, and kissing. They would have to avoid that, too, because it led to other kinds of trouble.

She walked downstairs, covered the cookies with plastic wrap, then grabbed her purse and headed for the front door. Seven minutes later she pulled up in front of the sheriff's station. Two minutes after that, she was escorted back to Gage's office.

As she walked down the long corridor, she found her heart fluttering a bit inside her chest. The odd sensation made her feel nervous and just a little out of breath.

Emotional reaction to their fight, she told herself. She was simply nervous that Gage might still be angry with her. She certainly wasn't *anticipating* seeing him again.

He was on the phone when she paused in the doorway to his office. Rather than focus on how good he looked in his khaki uniform, she glanced around at her surroundings.

Gage looked up and saw her. His expression stayed unreadable—something that seemed to happen a lot—

although she thought she might have caught the hint of a smile tugging at the corner of his mouth. He hesitated briefly before motioning her in.

She moved to a straight-backed chair in front of his desk, and perched on the edge. Gage wrapped up his conversation and set down the receiver. She swallowed. Now that she was here, she didn't know exactly what to say. Her situation wasn't helped by the continued fluttering of her heart, not to mention a noticeable weakness in her arms and legs. It was as if she'd just had a very large, very stiff shot of something alcoholic.

What on earth was wrong with her? Then, unbidden, the memory of the passion she and Gage had shared rose in her mind, filling her body with sensations and her imagination with possibilities.

She silently screamed at herself to get down to business. Namely, apologizing. There would be no sexual fantasies about Gage. Not now. Not ever! And she really meant it.

"Kari," he said, his voice low and sexy. *Really* sexy.

She shivered. "I, um, brought a peace offering." She pushed the plate of cookies across the desk toward him. "I figure we both overreacted, but I'm willing to be mature about it."

She was teasing, and hoped he would get the joke. Instead of saying anything, though, he peeled back the plastic wrap and pulled out a cookie. After taking a bite, he chewed.

"I can be mature," he said as he leaned back in his chair and smiled at her. "With motivation."

She relaxed in her seat. "Are these enough motivation?"

"Maybe. It might take another dozen or so."

"I'll see what I can do." The rapid beating of her heart continued, but the tension fled.

"I'm sorry," she said seriously.

"Me, too. Like you said, I overreacted."

"I said a lot of things…" She paused. "I'm sorry about saying I tested you and you failed. I didn't mean it like that. I was a kid back then and completely unprepared for a grown-up relationship. I ran away because I was scared and couldn't face you. I thought you'd be mad and try to get me to change my mind." She shrugged. "Like I said, not really mature. But I didn't plan to hurt you. I thought you'd come after me, and when you didn't, I decided you didn't really love me. I thought I was a placeholder. That any woman would have done as long as she fulfilled your need for a wife and mother for your kids."

Gage picked up a pen and turned it over in his hands. "It wasn't like that, Kari. Any of it. I wanted to go after you. Hell, I thought about it a hundred times a day. I missed you more than I can ever explain, but that didn't mean I couldn't see your side of things. I didn't want to understand why you'd run off, but in my heart I knew. I didn't think I had the right to drag you back. You needed to follow your dreams. I'd just hoped they would be the same as mine."

"They were…just not then. I needed time."

He nodded. They looked at each other, then away.

Kari pressed her lips together. "Maybe we could start over. Be friends?"

"I'd like that. We can hardly be strangers if you're dragging me over to work on your house every other minute."

"I did *not* drag you. You volunteered."

"That's your story."

She smiled. "You make me crazy."

"In the best way possible."

That was true. And speaking of being made crazy… She cleared her throat. "About the kissing."

He waved a hand. "You don't have to thank me. I didn't mind doing it."

"Gee, thanks. Actually, what I was going to say was that I think we need to avoid it. Kissing can lead to other things and those other things would provide a complication neither of us needs."

"Fine by me. I can control myself."

"So can I."

She was almost *sure* she was telling the truth. She should have been able to without a problem. It's just that she sort of wanted to know what it would be like to make love with Gage. In every other area of her life, he'd always been the best man she'd ever known. No doubt he would shine at lovemaking, too.

She knew he would be sensitive and considerate, two things that really mattered to her—what with her never actually having done, well, *that* before. Someone, somewhere was going to have to be her first time, and she'd always thought Gage would be really good at that. Right up until he freaked out when she told him that she was still a virgin.

Rather than tread on dangerous ground, she changed the subject. "I don't remember the sheriff's station being this big."

He grinned. "How many times were you in it before?"

She laughed. "Okay. Never."

"We have a contract to patrol state-owned land. Several of the small towns hire us to take care of them, as well. The department has more than doubled since you left. I have some other plans for expansion. More territory and more officers means a bigger budget. We can qualify for some federal grants and upgrade equipment, stay ahead of the bad guys."

He looked so strong and sure sitting in his chair. A man in charge of his kingdom.

"You're good at what you do, aren't you," she said.

"If I'm not, I won't get reelected."

"I doubt that's going to happen. Something tells me that you'll be sheriff of Possum Landing for a very long time."

"It's what I want."

She envied how he'd always known that. She'd had to search for what she wanted. "Speaking of wants and dreams, I'm heading up to Dallas in the morning. I have an interview."

"Good luck with that."

"Thanks."

She waited, kind of hoping he might express a little regret that she was leaving, but of course he didn't. Which made sense. After all, he knew her stay in town was temporary. He wasn't about to forget that, or start acting surprised when she had interviews in other places. Expecting anything else was really foolish and he knew better than to be that.

"I'll be back on Saturday," she said, rising.

Obviously, with her mental state, she had better head home fast. Before she said or did something she would regret. Like throw herself at him. What if he rejected her? She glanced around at the glass walls and everyone who could see in. Actually she would be in more trouble if he didn't reject her.

"I'll see you then," he said. "You'll dazzle them, Kari."

"Thanks. I'll do my best. 'Bye."

She waved and left his office, then returned to the entrance. The young deputy who had driven her home walked by. He nodded politely and called her ma'am, which made her feel old.

Once outside, she breathed in the afternoon heat and was grateful she'd driven. Any walk longer than ten feet would cause her to sweat through her clothes in about forty seconds. Now, if only she could hire a little elf to go turn on her car and start the air-conditioning. That would be heavenly.

No elf appeared, but just as Kari was about to open her car door, she heard someone call her name. Not Gage, unfortunately. This was a female someone. Kari's body tensed and her shoulders hunched up. Great. Just what she needed.

Still, she forced herself to smile pleasantly as she turned and saw Daisy walking toward her.

The pretty reporter wore a skirt tight enough to cut off the circulation to her shapely legs. An equally snug shirt emphasized large breasts that instantly made Kari feel like a thirteen-year-old still waiting for puberty. Okay, yes, she was tall and slender and she'd been a model, but that didn't change the fact that she was a scant 34B, with hips as wide as a twelve-year-old boy's.

Still, Kari had posture on her side, so she squared her shoulders and forced herself to think tall, elegant, I've-been-in-a-national-magazine type thoughts.

"Hi, Daisy," she said with a big ol' Texas-size smile. "Nice to see you again."

"You, too."

The curvaceous bombshell paused on the sidewalk by the front of Kari's car and gave her a look that could only be called pitying. "This must be so hard for you," she said.

Kari had a feeling Daisy didn't mean the heat, although that was plenty difficult to adjust to. "I'm not sure what you're talking about," she said when she couldn't think of anything else.

Daisy sighed heavily. "Gage, of course. You're still sweet on him. I saw the plate of cookies you took in to the sheriff's office just now. I was across the street getting my nails done."

Kari nodded without turning. She could feel herself flushing, even though she knew she had nothing to be embarrassed about.

Daisy blinked her long lashes. "The thing is, Kari, Gage doesn't go back. He never has. He stays friends with his old girlfriends, but nothing more. And believe you me, more than one girl has tried to get that horse back in the barn." She lowered her voice conspiratorially. "Can you blame them? Gage Reynolds is a catch with a capital *C*. But once things are over, they stay over. What with you being gone and all, I didn't think you knew. I just don't want to see you get hurt."

Kari doubted Daisy's motivation, if not her information. Somehow, she couldn't see the other woman staying up nights worrying about Kari's pain or lack thereof.

"I appreciate the tip," she said, dying to make a move toward her car but not wanting to be rude. She wondered how the very passionate kisses she and Gage had shared fit in with Daisy's revelation. At the same time, she couldn't help smiling at the mental image of him as a runaway horse to be recaptured.

A thought suddenly occurred to her. She glanced at the petite beauty standing on the sidewalk. Something twisted in her stomach and made her swallow hard.

"I didn't know," she said slowly, finally putting all the pieces together.

And she hadn't. Daisy's interest in Gage, her warning Kari away. The fact that Daisy was divorced.

"Didn't know what?" Daisy asked.

Kari felt trapped. "That you're interested in him." What she was thinking was "in love," but she didn't want to say that.

Daisy shrugged. "I am. I won't deny it. He's a good man and there aren't many of those around. I know. I was married to a real jerk, which explains my divorce."

Kari shifted uncomfortably. She didn't want Daisy

saying too much. Somehow it felt wrong. Guilt blossomed inside her. Here she'd been playing fast and loose with an ex-boyfriend, while Daisy had been… What? She didn't know Daisy's position on Gage.

"Are you in love with him?" she asked before she could stop herself.

Oddly enough, Daisy laughed. "Love? I don't think so. I've been in love and it was nothing but trouble. I like Gage a lot. I think we could have a successful marriage, and that's what matters to me. I'm thinking with my head and not any other body part. Not this time. I want a steady man who'll come home when he says and be a decent father to our kids. That man is Gage."

Kari couldn't disagree with her assessment of Gage, but Daisy's plan sounded so cold-blooded, which wasn't Gage's style.

"Does Gage share your feelings on the subject?" she asked.

"No. Like most men, he thinks falling in love makes everything hunky-dory. Which is fine with me. He can love me all he wants. I'll be the sensible one in the relationship." Daisy's eyes narrowed. "So don't for a moment think you can waltz back in here and pick up where you left off."

"It never crossed my mind," Kari said honestly.

"Good. I intend to win him. I just need a little time."

"I'm sure things will work out perfectly." Kari itched to get back in her car and drive away. More than that, she wished this conversation had never taken place.

The other woman sighed. "Don't take this personally, but I wish you'd never come back."

Kari was starting to have the same wish. She wasn't sure if she felt sorry for Gage or not. He was a big, strong guy—he should be able to handle Daisy. She also felt unsettled, but couldn't say why. Nor did she know what to say to end the conversation.

Finally she opened her car door. "For what it's worth," she said, tossing her purse onto the passenger seat, "I'm not back. Not permanently. So you don't have to worry about me."

"Oh, I didn't plan to."

Daisy waggled her fingers, then turned and headed for the sheriff's office. Kari considered calling out "good luck," but she knew in her heart that she would be lying.

"I don't know. Australia." Edie fingered the glossy travel brochure in front of her. "It's very far."

John, her fiancé, smiled indulgently. "Travel does tend to take one away from one's regular world. That's the point."

Edie rolled her eyes. "I know that. I just never thought…" Her voice trailed off. "Australia," she repeated softly.

Gage watched her from his place on the opposite side of the kitchen table. He'd joined his mother and John for dinner. Once the plates had been cleared, John had pulled out several brochures for trips to exotic places. He and Edie had yet to pick a honeymoon destination.

As Gage sipped his coffee, he couldn't help being

pleased with his mother's happiness. His father's death had nearly destroyed her. For a while he'd worried that he was going to lose her, as well. Eventually, she'd started to heal. But she hadn't returned to anything close to normal until she'd met John.

Physically, John wasn't anything like Gage's father, Ralph. The retired contractor was several inches shorter, stocky to Ralph's lean build, and blond with blue eyes to Ralph's dark coloring. But he was a good man with a generous nature and a loving heart. He'd wanted to sweep Edie off her feet and marry her that first month. Instead, he'd courted her slowly, giving her all the time she'd needed. It had taken over a year for her to agree to marry him, but since she'd admitted her feelings, they'd been inseparable.

While their budding romance had been strange to Gage, he'd tried to stay open to the idea. He'd quickly come to see that John wasn't trying to take anyone's place. And his mother deserved a chance at happiness.

"After touring Australia, we board the cruise ship. There are stops in Singapore, Hong Kong and other parts of China before heading to Japan. We'll fly back from there."

Edie shook her head. "Of course it sounds lovely." She glanced at her fiancé and smiled lovingly. "I won't even mention that it will be very expensive."

John gave a playful growl. "Good."

"I've always wanted to see that part of the world," she said wistfully.

"Then, you should say thank you, give your fiancé a big kiss and start making plans," Gage said easily. "Go for it, Mama."

They could both afford the time the long trip would take, and John had retired a millionaire. Even after settling money on his daughters and grandchildren, there was still plenty to keep him and his new wife in style.

Edie glanced from him to John, then nodded tentatively.

John grinned. "Where's that kiss your son suggested you give me?"

She brushed his mouth with hers.

Gage sipped at his coffee again. There had always been good times around this table. Years before, when his father was still alive, they'd often talked long into the night. Ralph had been devoted to his wife in many ways, but he'd been a stubborn man who didn't bend on many things. He hadn't liked to travel, and Edie's pleas to see if not the world, then parts of the country, went ignored.

Ralph had been born and bred in Possum Landing, and as far as he was concerned, a man couldn't do better. Gage knew he had a little of his father in him. He loved the town where he'd been born, and he never wanted to live anywhere else. Unlike his father, though, he hadn't made Possum Landing his whole world. He enjoyed going to different places. He supposed that was because he was also his mother's son.

Edie opened the brochure and spread it over the kitchen table. "I can't believe we're going to do this. Gage, look. We can take a trip to the Australian outback. Oh! There's snorkeling on the Great Barrier Reef."

"Watch out for sharks," he teased.

She gave him a loving smile and returned her attention to the pictures.

While his mother and John planned their trip, Gage stared out the open window into the night. He hadn't been very good company tonight, probably because he felt distracted. He didn't want to admit the cause of the problem, but he knew exactly what it was. Or rather who.

Kari.

She was back from her interview. Her trip had taken her away for three days, but she'd returned that morning. He'd seen her car. While he'd told himself that her comings and goings didn't matter to him, he'd acknowledged an inner relief at knowing she was once again in the house next door.

Trouble, he told himself grimly. Way too much trouble.

He knew at some point he was going to see her. No doubt he would continue to help her with the work she was doing on her grandmother's house. But something had changed between them. He didn't know if it was the fight or what had happened right before the fight. Passion had ignited and they'd both nearly gone up in flames. After all this time, he wouldn't have thought that was possible.

He finished his coffee, then stood and stretched. "It seems to me you lovebirds need to be alone," he teased.

Edie looked up. "Oh, Gage. Don't go. Are we ignoring you?"

He circled around the table, bent down and kissed her cheek. "You're planning your honeymoon,

Mama. I don't think you need your grown son hang-
ing around while you do that.''

He shook John's hand. ''Don't let her talk you into
a dark cabin in the ship's hold. She'll try.''

John grinned. ''Don't I know it. But I'm going to
insist on a suite.''

''Oh, John. That would be *so* expensive.''

The men shared a quick look that spoke of their
mutual affection for Edie.

Before leaving, Gage headed for the trash container
under the sink.

''You don't have to do that,'' John told him. ''I'll
take it out later.''

Gage shook his head. ''Don't sweat it. I have years
of practice. Besides, once you two are married, I plan
to let you take over all the chores.''

''It's a deal.''

Gage called out a good-night and walked out the
back door. The porch light illuminated his way. He
whistled tunelessly as he went to the trash can and
pulled off the lid. He was about to set the plastic bag
inside when he saw a beautiful cloth box resting on
several paper bags. While the floral print made him
want to gag, he recognized the container. His mother
kept pictures and other treasures inside. She'd had it
for as long as he could remember. Why would she be
throwing it out now?

Must be a mistake, he thought as he took it out of
the trash can and put the kitchen bag in its place. He
set the lid down and turned toward the house. But at
the bottom porch step, he stumbled slightly. The cloth
box went flying out of his hands, hit the next step up

and tipped open. Dozens and dozens of pictures spilled out onto the concrete.

Gage swore under his breath. As he bent to retrieve them, he recognized old photos of his mother, back when she was young. So damn beautiful, he thought as he started to pick them up. He saw her with Ralph and with her family. There were several—

Gage frowned as he shuffled through the pictures. There was his mother with a man he didn't recognize. At first he dismissed the pictures as taken before she'd married, but there was a wedding ring on her finger. Yet the man had his arm around her in a way that implied they were more than just friends. The man—

Gage stared at him. He was a stranger, yet there was something familiar about him. Gage picked up more pictures and flipped through them. The man appeared in several different shots. Always close to Gage's mother. Always looking pleased about something.

And then he got it. The man looked like Quinn, Gage's brother. Now that Gage looked closer, he saw a lot of himself in the man, too. So he *must* be a relative. But who?

The back door opened. "I didn't hear your truck start," his mother said. "Is there—" She gasped.

He glanced up and saw the color drain from her face. She pressed a hand to her mouth. Her eyes widened, and for a second he thought she was going to faint.

"Mama?"

She shook her head. "Dear God," she whispered. "I threw those out."

"I know. I saw the box. You always kept your treasures in it. I thought it was a mistake." But looking at her stricken expression he realized it hadn't been anything of the sort.

Something went cold inside him. Suddenly he wished he'd never picked up the box. He could be home by now. But instead of backing away, he held up a picture of the stranger with his mother.

"Who is this guy?"

She stared at him as if he held a gun. "S-someone I used to know." Her low voice was barely audible.

Gage had the sensation of walking through a minefield.

"Who is he? He looks a lot like Quinn, and I guess a little like me. Is he a relative? An uncle?"

He kept asking even though she didn't answer. He asked because if he didn't, if he allowed himself to think anything, he might figure out something he didn't want to know.

John stepped outside. He took one look at the pictures, then pulled Edie close. "It's all right," he murmured to her.

Gage's gut tightened. John knew. Whatever the secret was, the other man knew. Suddenly Gage had to know, too.

"Who is he?" he repeated.

Tears spilled from her eyes. She turned to her fiancé and clung to him, her entire body shaking with her sobs. Gage hadn't felt afraid in a long time, but he felt a cold uncertainty now.

"John?"

"We should all go inside," the older man said quietly. "Let's talk about this inside."

"No. Tell me now."

John stroked Edie's hair. "Gage, there are things…" He broke off and sighed. "Edie, what do you want me to do?"

His mother looked at John. Whatever the man saw in her eyes caused him to nod. He turned to Gage.

"Please come inside, Gage. I don't want to tell you like this."

"I'm not going anywhere until you answer the question. Who is this man?"

John took a deep breath. "He's your father."

Chapter Eight

Kari paced the length of the parlor, pausing every trip to glance out the front window to see if Gage had returned yet. She knew that he was having dinner at his mom's tonight and that she could stop pacing because as long as she stayed at the front of the house, she would hear his truck approach. But logic didn't seem to eliminate her need to keep walking.

She wanted to see him, she admitted to herself. She wanted to talk to him and joke with him and just plain be in the same room with him. She'd only been gone three days, but it felt longer than that. Somehow, reconnecting with Gage would make her homecoming more complete.

Well, not a homecoming, she told herself firmly. This wasn't home and she wasn't back. It's just that she was in Possum Landing temporarily and he was a part of that. Or something.

She crossed to the window again and stared out into the night. She had so much she wanted to tell him. Her interview had gone really well. She'd met with the principal and several of the teachers. The following day she'd met with a small committee from the board of education. On her second interview with the principal, the woman had hinted that an offer more than likely would be forthcoming. So things were going really great. That's why she wanted to see Gage. She wanted him to help her celebrate. Or something.

"Where are you?" she muttered aloud, dropping the curtain and resuming her circuit of the parlor. The restlessness had returned and with it a longing for something she couldn't define or name. It filled her until she wanted to jump out of her skin.

Just when she knew she couldn't stand it one more second, she heard his truck pull into the driveway next door. Kari ran to the front door and pulled it open, then hurried across the porch and down the front steps. Her heart quickened, as did her footsteps.

As he stepped down from the cab, she crossed the last few feet between them. They had agreed to no more kissing, but was it permissible to throw herself in his arms? Because that's what she felt like doing. Just launching herself in his general direction and—

He turned toward her. Light from the house spilled into the night, illuminating a bit of the driveway and part of his face. She came to a stop as if she'd hit a brick wall. Something had happened—she saw it in his eyes. Something bad.

"Gage?"

He stared at her, his expression bleak, his mouth set. Instead of speaking, he shook his head, then walked toward his house.

Kari hesitated, not sure what to do. Finally she followed him up the steps, so much like those at her grandmother's, into a house that mirrored hers.

Same front room, same hallway, same stairs—only reversed and modernized. Several floor lamps provided light. She had a quick impression of hardwood floors, overstuffed furniture and freshly painted walls, before Gage captured her attention by crossing to a cabinet at the end of the parlor. He opened it, pulled out a bottle of scotch and poured himself a drink. He downed it in two gulps, poured another and moved to the sofa, where he sank down.

"Help yourself," he said, his voice low and hoarse.

She watched him take another gulp, then set the half-full glass on the wooden coffee table, leaned back and closed his eyes.

Fear flickered inside her. Instead of claiming the drink he'd offered, she headed for the sofa and settled next to him. She was close enough to study him, but far enough away that she didn't crowd him.

After a few minutes of silence, she lightly touched his arm. "Want to talk about it?"

He shrugged. "I don't know what to say."

"Is everyone all right? Your mom? Quinn? Did you hear from the government?"

He turned toward her and opened his eyes. Anguish

darkened the brown irises. He looked like a man who had been to hell and faced the devil.

"No one's dead," he said flatly. "At least, no one who wasn't dead before."

She didn't know what to say to that. But without knowing the problem, how could she help? Or could she? He hadn't told her to go away, which relieved her, but she had a bad feeling that if he did finally spill the beans, she wasn't going to be any happier for knowing.

He rubbed his temples, then reached for his drink. After finishing it, he set the glass back on the table.

"I've only been really furious once before in my life," he said, his voice still lacking expression or emotion. "I've been mad and angry, just like everyone else. But I'm talking about that inner rage that burns hot and makes a man want to take on the world."

She stared at him. He didn't look angry. He didn't look anything.

"When was that?" she asked.

"When you left."

She winced.

He shrugged. "It's the truth. I read and reread your note about a hundred times, then I went and got skunk drunk. I decided to go after you. It's a little fuzzy now, but I think I had this plan to chase down your bus and drag you off. I was going to tell you exactly what I thought of you. I knew better, but I wanted to do it, anyway. I'd never been so angry in my life."

She swallowed. "What happened?"

"I got lucky. When I crashed, I only hurt myself.

I totaled the car and walked away with a few scars.'' He glanced at her. "I learned my lesson. I may get drunk tonight, but I won't be driving.''

"Okay.''

She was no closer than she had been to getting at the problem. No one was dead and he didn't plan on getting drunk, then chasing someone down in a car.

"If you're keeping me company, it's going to be a long night,'' he said. "You might as well pour me another and get yourself one, too. You're going to need it.''

Kari took his advice. She carried his glass back to the cabinet, got one for herself and poured for both of them. When she returned to the sofa, she said, "Tell me what happened.''

Gage stared into his drink. What had happened? Nothing. Everything. How was he to explain that his entire world had shifted on its axis? Nothing he knew as true was as it had been before. Nothing was as it had been just an hour before. In a heartbeat—with less than half a dozen words—everything had changed.

"I was at my mom's for dinner,'' he began slowly, not looking at her, not wanting her to see inside of him, not wanting to know what she was thinking. "When I left, I took the trash out, like I always do. There was a box in the trash can outside. A cloth-covered one my mom had kept for years. She always stored important pictures and stuff in it, so I thought it must be a mistake. I started to carry it back inside, but I tripped on the steps and it went flying. Everything fell out. There were pictures inside.''

He fell silent. His brain didn't seem to be working. He could speak the words, but he wasn't thinking them first. They simply came out on their own. He thought about what had happened, but it was as if he were viewing a movie. That man on the stairs wasn't him. The woman wasn't his mother. They hadn't had that conversation.

"A man." He continued before he could stop himself. "My mother with a man."

Kari leaned close and touched his arm again. He liked that. She was warm and steady in his cold, spinning world.

"She had an affair?"

He nodded.

Beside him, Kari sighed. "I know that's a tough one. You have this idea of your parents' marriage and it's one in which they both never mess up. You must have been really shocked."

She didn't understand. Probably because he hadn't told her all of it. The most important part. The part that had torpedoed his past and dropped land mines in his future.

"John knew," he said flatly. "He came out on the porch. She started to cry and couldn't speak, but he told me." Against his will he turned to look at Kari. "The man in the picture is my father."

She stared at him. Her eyes widened, her lips parted and color drained from her face. "Gage," she breathed.

He nodded slightly. "Yeah. I can't believe it, either. It can't be true. My dad—I mean Ralph." He shuddered.

None of this made sense. It would never make sense. Anger filled him again. Anger and pain—a deadly combination. Only, this time he wasn't going to get drunk and go tearing down city streets. This time he was going to sit here and do nothing until it all went away.

"Your father," she said.

"Which one?"

"Your real one. Ralph. I don't understand. Your parents were so in love. Everyone knew it. They spent all their time together. They were always talking and laughing. I know your mom. She's not the kind of woman who would…" Her voice trailed off.

Gage knew what she meant. He would never have guessed his mother was the kind of woman who would have an affair and then pass her bastard off as her husband's kid. And he could never see his father allowing it.

"How did it happen?" she asked.

"I don't know. I didn't stick around long enough to ask questions." Instead, he'd walked out, the sound of his mother's sobs following him to his truck.

"I don't want it to be true," he admitted quietly. "Not any of it. If I'm not my father's son…"

Who was he? Five generations of Reynolds living in Possum Landing. He'd always taken pride in that. He'd made his history a part of who he was. Except, that wasn't his history anymore. He didn't have one—just lies.

Kari shifted close and tucked her arm around his. She leaned her head on his shoulder. "Oh, Gage. I don't know what to say. I have so many questions, but no way to make you feel better. I'm sorry."

He didn't say anything, nor did he move away. Having Kari next to him felt right. Her touch and her words alone weren't enough to make him feel better, but that didn't mean he wanted her to move away. He needed the connection to her tonight more than he ever had.

They sat in silence for a long time.

"He's Quinn's father, too," Gage said finally. "I could see the resemblance in the pictures."

Kari raised her head. "Quinn's father? But then the affair was ongoing. For at least a couple of years. How is that possible?"

"I don't know. While the guy in the picture looked familiar because of Quinn looking so much like him, I've never seen him before. I'm guessing he's not from around here."

He couldn't comprehend his mother having a brief affair, let alone something that lasted long enough to produce two children. Where the hell had his father, Ralph, been in all this? Gage would have bet his life that his dad— He swore, *not* his father. He didn't know his father. Damn. He would have bet his life that Ralph wouldn't tolerate Edie being unfaithful, no matter how much he loved her. So what had happened?

The phone rang. He didn't move.

Kari turned her head toward the sound. "Aren't you going to get that?"

"No."

"It's probably your mom, or maybe John."

Gage shrugged. He didn't want to talk to either of them.

Kari started to say something, but the start of the message cut her off. The sound of his voice filled the room.

"It's Gage. I'm not in. Leave a message at the tone."

"G-Gage—?" His mother's voice broke. "Are you there? I'm so s-sorry. I know you're upset and—" She began to cry.

Kari got up and walked to the phone. He didn't try to stop her because it didn't matter. She and his mother could talk all night and it wouldn't change anything.

Without Kari beside him, the anger burned hotter and brighter. He didn't like being afraid, so he sank into rage, instead. It was safer, easier. The sense of betrayal nearly overwhelmed him. He knew that whatever his mother had to say, whatever the excuses might be, they weren't going to be enough. He would never forgive her.

When Kari returned, she sat on the coffee table, her knees between his. She leaned toward him and took his hands in hers.

"Your mom wanted to know that you're okay," she told him. "I said you were still in shock."

Her blue eyes were steady as she looked at his face. Despite his pain and confusion, he thought she was one of the most beautiful women he'd ever known. Her wide eyes, her full mouth, her perfect skin.

She squeezed his fingers. "She wants to talk to you."

Rage returned. "No," he said flatly.

"You're going to have to do it sometime."

"Why?"

"To get your questions answered."

"I don't have any."

"Gage, of course you do. Too many questions. Edie said she has to explain. There are things you don't understand."

"You think?" he asked bitterly.

Kari continued to hold his hands. "Your relationship with your mother has always been extremely important to you. After all these years, you're not going to turn your back on her regardless of how angry you are right now."

"Want to bet?"

"Absolutely. I know you. You need to hear her out. You need to know and understand the truth. There are things you have to be told."

He jerked his hands free and glared at her. "Like the fact that the man I thought was my father isn't? I already know that one."

"Biology doesn't change the memories. Your father loved you very much."

"I don't know if my father even knows I'm alive."

"Ralph is your father in every sense of the word."

"Not anymore." Not ever.

Kari glared at Gage. She hated when he got stubborn. He was like a giant steer in the middle of the road. All the prodding in the world wasn't going to get him to move until he decided he was good and ready. Only, being stubborn this time was going to hurt both him and Edie.

Kari didn't know what had happened thirty-plus years ago. Nor had Edie explained how she'd come to be pregnant by a man other than her husband. But Kari knew there had to be a darn good explanation, and if Gage would stop being angry for one second, he would figure it out, too.

But she couldn't bring herself to be upset with him. Not when he looked so broken. The big, strong man she'd always known still sat in front of her, but behind his eyes lurked something dark and lonely. Something that cried out to her.

Impulsively she leaned toward him, sliding to the edge of the coffee table. She could just stretch her hands far enough to reach his shoulders. When she touched the cloth of his shirt, she drew him toward her.

He didn't cooperate, which was just so like him. How difficult could one man be?

"Work with me, here," she said in frustration, then moved to the sofa and knelt beside him.

She rested her hands on his shoulders and brushed his mouth with hers. The kiss came from a need to comfort and connect.

For a second he didn't respond. But just as she was about to move back, his arms came around her waist and he hauled her up against him. Her knee sank in between the cushions, causing her to almost lose her balance. But before she could fall, he turned her slightly, shifting her weight until she sat on his lap, her body angled toward his.

It wasn't exactly what she'd had in mind when she'd first kissed him, but now that she was here, she found that being cradled next to Gage was a really nice way to spend an evening. Especially when he slightly opened his mouth and swept his tongue across her lower lip.

Suddenly the tension in the room shifted. It was no longer about an external situation, but about what was growing between *them*. Hot tension. Sexual tension. Need. Desire.

Her hold on his shoulders changed from gentle to intense. The compassionate ache inside her became a very different kind of ache. She wanted to offer a whole lot more than just comfort.

She parted her lips to admit him, then stroked her tongue against his when he accepted the invitation. He wrapped his arms around her and pulled her even closer to his chest. Then his hands were everywhere— stroking her back, her hips, her legs. In turn she touched his face, feeling rough stubble, then the smooth silk of his hair. She tried to press herself against him, but in their current positions it was impossible.

Still, the deep, powerful, passionate kisses took some of the sting out of that. When he retreated, she followed, only to have him close his mouth around her tongue and suck. Shivers raced through her. Warm, liquid heat stirred between her legs. Her breasts swelled inside her bra as her nipples tightened.

She thought he might have noticed because he moved his hand along the outside of her leg to her hips, then up her waist and rib cage to her breasts. Once there, he settled his palm over her curves. The delightful weight made her squirm. The shivering increased, as did her desire to have him touch her all over…without clothes as a barrier.

The concept should have shocked her, but it didn't. This was Gage—the man she'd always trusted. If he wanted to make love tonight, she would only encourage the idea. She'd never been sure with anyone else, but she was sure with him.

So she arched into his touch and moaned softly when he brushed his thumb against her tight nipple. Against her hip—the one nestling into his groin—she felt something hard pressing into her. She wiggled to get a little closer.

Suddenly he moved her, shifting her so she had to scramble to keep her balance. He set her on her feet, then rose, as well. Questions filled his eyes, but so did need and wanting.

"Kari?"

She leaned in to him and ran her hands up and down his strong chest. It seemed to be the answer he was looking for. He drew her close and kissed her again, this time plunging inside of her and taking what he wanted. She reveled in his desire. Heat filled her, melting her until it was difficult to remain standing.

He cupped her face, then slipped his fingers through her hair. He broke the kiss, started it again, then stopped.

When she looked at him, she saw the darkness was gone. Instead, humor brightened his expression.

"I'm trying to stop long enough to get us upstairs," he said. "I have a very comfortable bed, not to mention protection. But I can't keep my hands off you."

"Who says you have to?" she asked as she turned toward the stairs. "Last one upstairs has to strip for the winner."

Gage chuckled, then moved after her. Halfway up the stairs, he grabbed her by the waist and drew her to him. They were on different steps, and she shrieked when she almost lost her balance.

"It's okay," he whispered, picking her up and turning so that she dangled in front of him while he faced the bottom of the staircase.

"What on earth are you doing?" she demanded.

"Making sure I get there first." He spoke directly into her ear. "I like to watch."

She barely had time to absorb his words before he reached the landing.

"I win," he said, releasing her so that her feet touched solid flooring again. He clicked on a light.

She sidled away and glanced at him from under her lashes. *I like to watch.* His words made her both excited and a little uncomfortable.

"Gage, I don't know if I can—"

He captured her hand and raised it to his mouth, where he planted tiny, damp kisses on the inside of her wrist. "I know. It's okay. I was teasing."

"Are you sure?" She looked at him anxiously. "I want to do what—" She cleared her throat. "I just couldn't…"

This was probably the time to tell him that she was a virgin, although she had a bad feeling that if she did, he would stop. Which wasn't what she wanted.

And while she fit the technical description of someone who had never had actual penetration, she'd played around some. It's not as if she'd never seen a naked man before. She'd even climaxed once, although that sure hadn't been the experience she'd been hoping for.

"You don't have to strip for me," he said gently as he touched her cheek. "We can save that for next time."

Relief filled her. "I'm not sure I should commit to that, either. Maybe you should strip for me next time."

"It's a deal."

He stared at her, then bent down and kissed her. As his tongue slipped into her mouth, he cupped her breasts, angling his hands so he could rub her tight nipples. The combination of sensations made her knees nearly give way. She had to hold on to him to keep upright.

Then they were moving. As he kissed her and touched her, he urged her backward, heading them toward the large bedroom at the end of the hallway. But before they were halfway there, he broke the kiss long enough to pull off her T-shirt. Then she felt his hands on her breasts with one less layer between them.

His fingers touched the top of her breasts, his thumbs teasing the nipples while his palms supported her curves. He was warm, gentle and very sexy, she thought dreamily as they started to move again.

This time when they stopped, she kicked off her sandals. Gage had something else in mind. He reached for the fastening on her bra and undid it. The wisp of lace seemed to vanish into thin air. Then his hands were back, but on bare flesh this time.

She arched her head as he cupped her, stroked her, teased her. His skin was slightly rough—not enough to hurt her, but just enough to be…delicious. As he played with her breasts, he kissed along her jaw, then licked the sensitive skin just below her ear. She moaned in delight as pleasure swept through her body.

"I want to touch you everywhere," he whispered in her ear. "I want to touch you and taste you and listen to your breathing change. I want to take you to the edge and back, until you don't have any choice but to fall over. Then I want to catch you and make it happen again and again."

She shivered at his words and began to wonder how much farther it was to the bedroom. They began to move. When her bare feet felt the change from hardwood to carpet, she knew they were close. Gage moved away long enough to turn on a lamp on the nightstand and pull back the covers. Then he returned to her side. But he didn't touch her breasts. Instead, he knelt on the floor and went to work on her shorts.

They came off easily, as did her panties. In a matter of seconds, she was naked. Before she could be embarrassed, he pressed a kiss to her belly and began to move lower.

Kari had an idea of his ultimate destination and it worried her. Someone else had done that to her once. All her friends raved about the glories of oral sex, while she had found it embarrassing and more than a little painful. All that sucking and biting had left her bruised and seeking escape. But how to say that without sounding like an idiot?

She put her hand on his head to get his attention, but before she could speak, he reached his goal. He used his fingers to part her slightly, then leaned in close and licked the most sensitive part of her.

Liquid fire shot through her. There was no other way to describe it, she thought, more than a little dazed. The slow, gentle movement of his tongue made her want to moan, or even scream. If he didn't do that again, she wouldn't be able to survive.

Fortunately he did do it again…and again. He licked and pressed and kissed so very lightly. She found herself wanting more. There was also the issue of her standing, which meant she couldn't part her legs enough. But she didn't want him to stop so that she could climb onto the mattress. It was a dilemma unlike any she'd ever faced.

Gage solved it for her by shifting her onto the edge of the bed. She fell back, legs spread shamelessly, her entire body begging him to do more and more until she got so lost in the pleasure that she couldn't find her way out.

He chuckled softly as he moved close, draping her legs over his shoulders. She was exposed and completely at his mercy. She couldn't remember ever being so vulnerable in her life. She felt wonderful.

Then he licked her again, and she felt even better than wonderful. He knew exactly how to touch her, how to make her breathing stop, how to make her scream. He moved faster, then slower, controlling the building passion, making her get so close she couldn't help but release, then he pulled her back at the last second and left her panting.

As he worked his magic between her legs, he reached up and touched her breasts. He cupped the curves and lightly pinched her nipples. The combination of sensations made it impossible for her to catch her breath. Then he was moving faster and faster, and she knew that this time if he stopped she would have a heart attack and die right there in his bed and—

She screamed. Her cry of pleasure filled the room as he took her to the edge and gently pushed her out into the warm, sensual darkness. Shudders raced through her body. Heat filled her as her release went on for a lifetime, rising and falling, but never, ever ending.

It was better than anything she'd ever read about. Obviously she'd been doing something very wrong until this point.

With a sigh of contentment, she floated back to reality and found herself lying on Gage's bed. He'd shifted her fully onto the mattress and was in the process of taking off his clothes. She looked at him as he undressed, taking in the firm muscles and, as he dropped his boxers, the size of him.

Kari searched her feelings and knew this was right for her. There wasn't a doubt in her mind that he would stop if she asked him to. But instead of questions or uncertainty, a little voice inside whispered only one thing—

It's about time!

Gage watched Kari watching him. She seemed lost in thought, then gave a slow smile. "What's so funny?" he asked as he reached for the box of condoms in his nightstand.

"I was just thinking that we've waited a long time to do this. So far, I have to say the experience has been extraordinary."

"I'll do my best to make sure it continues to be so."

"I have every confidence."

He wasn't so sure. Pleasuring her had been easy. He liked everything about her body, from her slender curves to the way she tasted. But once he was on top of her and inside her it was going to be a different story. He had a bad feeling that he wasn't going to last all that long. He felt as if he could explode at any second.

He slipped onto the bed next to her and touched her flat stomach. "So this is where I tell you it's been a really long time since I've been with anyone. Add that to the fact that I used to spend hours fantasizing about making love with you, and we've got trouble. If you're hoping for a stellar performance, you may have to wait for round two."

She leaned on one elbow and kissed him. "You say the sweetest things. Did you really fantasize about me?"

He chuckled. "All those evenings spent kissing in the front seat of my car. Kissing and kissing and very little else. Of course I fantasized. I was so hard, I could barely walk—so what else could I do?"

"Maybe you'd like to take one of those fantasies out for a test drive."

Her words were all the invitation he needed. He slipped on the condom and positioned himself between her legs. He glanced at her perfect body, then shifted his gaze to her face. Her blue eyes stared back just as intently. He began to slip inside her.

She was hot, wet and tight. The combination didn't bode well for his self-control. He gritted his teeth and thought about all the paperwork on his desk. Then he moved on to the city council meeting about adding a traffic light. He was—

He swore silently as he continued to fill her. It was impossible to think of anything but how good she felt. He wanted to lose control. Which would take about two seconds.

No. Better to go slow the first time. He wanted it to be good for her. He—

He stopped suddenly at an unexpected barrier. What…?

But before he could think coherently enough to figure out what was wrong, Kari put her hands on his hips and drew him forward. At the same moment, she arched and made a request using a very bad word.

How was he supposed to refuse?

So he pushed into her, breaking through the barrier. At that second, she stiffened and gave a muffled cry. Only, it wasn't of pleasure. Her eyelids drifted closed. His heart sank.

Dammit all to hell. She'd been a virgin.

Chapter Nine

Gage started to withdraw, but before he could, Kari opened her eyes and clamped her hands on his hips.

"Don't," she whispered fiercely. "There's no reason to stop."

He could think of about fifty…or at least one really good one. But she was moving beneath him, urging him on.

"It's already done," she pointed out. "There's no going back."

Not exactly words he wanted to hear. Unfortunately he'd reached the point of no return, and one way or the other, his body was going to make sure he finished what he'd started. He decided to pull out, to not make things worse, but parts of him had other ideas. He'd barely started his retreat when the powerful rush of his release exploded from him, temporarily making rational thought impossible.

He pushed deep inside her until the last of the shudders faded, then withdrew. As he did, he was damn grateful he'd taken care of birth control.

He rolled off her without saying anything and headed for the bathroom. Once he settled next to her again, he closed his eyes and prayed fervently for no more surprises...at least not for the next twenty-four hours. He didn't think his heart would survive another one. But in the meantime there were the ramifications of the latest newsflash in his life.

He shifted until he could see Kari. She lay on her side of the bed, naked and studying him with a wary expression. As much as he wanted to remind her that she should have told him, that he should have been part of the decision-making process, he didn't want to turn her first time into something ugly. So he banked any lingering temper and remembered what it had felt like to make her climax. He recalled the taste of her skin and the soft sound of her cries. He smiled softly and touched her cheek.

"Want to tell me why?" he asked quietly.

"Why I'm a virgin? Why I chose you? Why now?"

"Any of those would be a good starting point."

Color stained her cheeks, leftover proof of her pleasure. Or maybe she was embarrassed. Her mussed hair framed her face, her mouth was swollen, her eyes were heavy lidded. She looked like a woman who had been well loved. She didn't look anything like a virgin.

She lifted one bare shoulder in a shrug. "I didn't set out to have this happen. I never intended to stay a virgin this long. It's just one of those things."

"Go on," he said, when she stopped talking.

"There's not much to say. I did date while I was in New York, but not all that much. Men who were obsessed with models terrified me, so I avoided anyone who seemed like a groupie. I was selective, cautious, and I moved slow. Most of them gave up on me before I had a chance to give in."

"Their loss."

She smiled slowly. "That's what I always said. I played around some, heavy petting, that sort of thing. But somehow, I never really got around to…you know." She shrugged again.

He wasn't sure what to make of her brief explanation. While he had always regretted not being her first, it had never occurred to him there might be a second chance for them.

"That explains why you were still a virgin," he said slowly. "But why now? Why with me?"

She stared at the bed, tracing a pattern with her finger. "I wanted my first time to be with someone I liked and respected. That's a more difficult combination to find than I would have thought. I didn't come home thinking we'd do what we ended up doing together, but tonight, when I knew you wanted me—" She cleared her throat, then continued. "It just seemed like the right thing to do."

No woman had ever shocked him so much in bed. He still wasn't sure what he felt. No way Kari would have set him up. But he was sure confused.

"I wish you'd told me," he said. "I would have done things differently if I'd known."

"Yeah, you would have run."

He grinned. "Darlin', this is Texas. We don't have any hills."

"What about in the Hill Country?"

"Bumps. They're glorified bumps."

She laughed softly, then her humor faded. "I thought you'd be mad. Or you'd change your mind. Or both."

He considered the possibilities. Had he known, would he have wanted to take on the responsibility of being Kari's first?

"I didn't want to make it a big deal," she said as if she could read his mind. "Are you mad?"

"No. Startled maybe."

Her mouth curved up at the corners. "I'll bet. If you could have seen the look on your face."

He didn't smile back. Instead, he moved close and drew her to him. What was done was done. He might not have controlled how it started, but he would make sure it ended well.

"I'm sorry I hurt you," he said.

"That comes with the territory," she said, snuggling closer still. "The rest of it was great."

"Thank you."

If nothing else, she'd taken his mind off his troubles. Now, in his bed, with both of them naked after just having made love, he refused to think about the other surprise in his life. He focused on the feel of Kari's bare skin and the scent of her body.

"Do you want me to go?" she asked suddenly.

"Go where?"

"Back to my place?"

He rubbed her back, then slipped his hand to her hip. "I would like whatever you would like. Do you want to spend the night?"

"Here?"

"Right here in this bed. Unless you're a cover hog. Then, you'll have to sleep in the guest room."

"I don't really know what I am," she admitted.

"Maybe it's time we found out."

She gave him a smile that could light up the sky. "Maybe it is."

He pulled up the covers and flicked out the light. Kari rested her head on his shoulder.

"Gage?" she said into the darkness.

"Yeah."

"You made my first time terrific. Thank you."

"You're welcome."

He held her tightly against him and listened to the sound of her breathing. If he'd been in possession of all the facts, maybe he wouldn't have chosen to sleep with Kari tonight, but now that it had happened, he couldn't find it in himself to regret it. Not for a minute.

Kari awoke sometime in the middle of the night. A bit of street light filtered in through a crack in the drapes. Gage lay beside her, but she couldn't hear his breathing, so she didn't know if he was awake or not.

Her body both tingled and ached. The remnants of amazing sexual pleasure lingered, but there was a faint soreness between her legs.

She turned toward Gage, studying the barely visible outline of his profile.

He could have been furious with her. After all, she hadn't warned him what he was getting into. In the end, he'd been sweet and funny and he'd made her feel really good. Not just about the sex, but about choosing him.

Her decision hadn't been conscious, she acknowledged. In light of what had been going on, it had seemed to be the logical thing to do. Being with him had felt right. She'd been afraid the actual act of making love would be awkward or embarrassing, but he'd made it all easy and exciting.

"Why aren't you asleep?" he asked unexpectedly.

She blinked. "How do you know I'm not?"

"I can hear you thinking."

She laughed. "Okay. Why aren't you sleeping?"

"Too much on my mind."

"Oh, Gage." She slid closer and placed her arm across his chest. "I wish I could help."

"Me, too. But I have to work things out for myself."

His tone indicated he didn't actually believe that was possible. She thought about telling him there wasn't anything to work out. He had to come to peace with his mother's revelation. However, she doubted he would appreciate the advice.

"Want to talk about it?" she asked.

"No. But thanks for offering."

"Want a massage?"

"No."

"Want me to talk dirty?"

He turned toward her. She thought she caught a glimpse of a smile. ''I have another suggestion. Turn over so you're facing the other way.''

She did as he requested, shifting until her back was to him. He moved behind her, spooning his body to hers. She felt his strong thighs pressing against hers and his chest heating her back. He wrapped an arm around her waist.

''Go to sleep, Kari,'' he whispered. ''Dream good dreams.''

''You, too.''

She had more to say, but suddenly it was very difficult to talk. Everything felt heavy, then light, then she didn't remember anything at all.

Kari awoke just after dawn to an empty bed and the smell of coffee. She was also naked and in Gage's bed.

Several thoughts occurred to her at once. First, it was daylight. It was one thing to not mind being naked in a man's bed while it was still night, but in the morning everything looked different. Her second thought was that she'd come over without even closing her front door, let alone locking it. While this was not a big deal in Possum Landing, she'd been in New York long enough to realize she'd behaved like a blockhead. Third...

Gage walked into the bedroom with two cups of coffee, chasing the third thing completely from her mind. Probably because he'd pulled on jeans. Jeans and nothing else.

Kari sat up, pulling the sheet with her, and stared

at his bare chest. Hair dusted the defined muscles, narrowing into a thin line that bisected his belly. He was tanned, strong and so masculine she would swear she could feel a swoon coming on.

The stubble darkening his jaw only added to his appeal. He looked dangerous and sexy, not to mention very yummy.

He smiled at her. "How did you sleep?"

"Good. Better than I would have thought. I was never one for spending the night."

His smile broadened. "That must be a virgin thing."

"Must be."

He handed her a mug of coffee and sat on the edge of the bed. "You okay?"

Suddenly shy, she studied the dark liquid before she sipped it. "Yes. Fine. Great."

"Kari?" His voice was a low growl.

She glanced up at him. "I'm fine," she repeated. "Are you okay with everything?"

"Yeah. Still dealing with the shock, but if you don't have any regrets, I don't either."

Relief filled her. "No regrets. I'll admit I should have told you. But I know you would have completely freaked, so I can't be sorry that I didn't."

"I'll give you that—but no more secrets, okay?"

She smiled. "That was my last big one."

He nodded. "Want to take a shower?"

"Sure." She put her mug on the nightstand. "I'll go first—or do you want to?"

He didn't answer. Instead he simply stared at her.

Kari blinked. Then heat flared on her face. *Shower,*

he'd said. *Do you want to take a shower?* She swallowed.

"Oh," she said in a tiny voice. "You mean together."

"Uh-huh. I have a big old-fashioned tub with a showerhead above it. Plenty of room for two."

"Oh." Oh my!

She had instant visions of them wet and naked and under a stream of hot water. Based on what had happened last night, she was sure whatever she imagined couldn't come close to the glories of reality. Any initial embarrassment would be worth the final result. After all, Gage was very good at what he did.

"Sure," she said, with more bravery than she actually felt. She threw back the covers and headed for the bathroom. "Give me five minutes to, uh, get ready."

"Sure."

She heard him chuckle behind her as she raced into the bathroom and closed the door. One minute to tinkle, one minute and thirty seconds to brush her teeth, one minute to wash the makeup off her face.

She turned on the hot water and let it run. As she'd hoped, Gage took the hint and entered the bathroom…sans clothing. Of course, all he'd had to pull off was jeans, but still, there he was naked and rather ready.

Were they going to— Could they actually do it in the shower? As she fretted logistics, he moved close enough to brush the hair off her forehead, then kissed her.

"You're thinking again. I can hear the gears creaking as they turn faster and faster."

"I can't help it. This is a new experience."

"You'll like it," he promised.

Somehow, she didn't doubt that.

He reached past her and adjusted the water, then stepped into the old-fashioned claw-foot tub. He held the curtain open for her as she stepped in beside him.

The master bath, like much of the house, had been completely refurbished. She wasn't sure, but she thought he might have broken through to the bedroom next door and taken about five feet of floor space. In her grandmother's bathroom, there wasn't this much room.

She was working out the construction details in her mind, when Gage directed her to stand beneath the spray. As warm water ran down the front of her body, he went to work on the other side. He lathered soap in his hands, then rubbed them over her shoulders and down her arms. He lathered her back, her fanny and her legs. Then he turned her toward him so she could rinse off.

While the warm spray sluiced down her skin, he leaned close and kissed her. She parted instantly for him, welcoming him, teasing him, tasting that appealing combination of mint and coffee. As he kissed her, he poured shampoo into his hands, then began to wash her hair. The combination of his tongue in her mouth and his fingers massaging her scalp was a sensual delight. She found herself swaying slightly, needing to rest her hands on his chest to steady herself.

He broke the kiss and had her lean her head back to rinse out the shampoo.

Hands made slick from soap glided over her skin. He circled her breasts, then massaged her nipples until they were hard and she was panting. Desire filled her. When he moved lower, she parted her legs to allow him access.

He soaped her gently, then rubbed lightly, as if aware parts of her were still a little tender. Then he reached above her and unfastened the showerhead. She noticed for the first time that it was on a hose. He lowered it and adjusted the spray to a lighter misting, then applied the warm water to her chest, her breasts, then even lower—between her legs.

She gasped. The pulsing water not only washed away soap, it vibrated against her most sensitive places. Tension swept through her, making her hold on to him with both hands. When he bent down and kissed her mouth, she kissed him back hard.

Their tongues danced together. Between her legs the water flowed just enough to excite, but not enough to take her over the edge. When he finally moved the showerhead back into place, she found herself trembling in anticipation of the next round.

"Your turn," she said, reaching for the soap.

She explored his back, taking her time over rippling muscles and a high, tight rear end that deserved a good nibbling. She made a mental note to take care of that soon. After rinsing him off, she had him turn so she could do the front.

Washing his hair proved something of a challenge as he was several inches taller than her, but she gave it her best shot, and he helped. Then she concentrated on the rest of him.

She massaged his chest, paying attention to his tight nipples. His breath caught when she brushed against them, so she did it several times. She moved lower and lower, dragging her soapy hands to his arousal jutting out toward her. Her fingers encircled him, moving lower, washing between his legs, rubbing back and forth. Just the act of touching him was enough to quicken her breathing. She still ached, but in a completely different way. She wanted him inside her. She wanted to make love with him again. She wanted—

He turned suddenly and rinsed off. "We'll be running out of hot water soon," he said. "I keep meaning to replace the old water heater, but so far I haven't been motivated. You might change that."

She stared at his back. That was it? They weren't going to… But he was hard. She was wet. They had time, means, opportunity and plenty of desire.

He turned off the water and she nearly screamed. Then Gage turned back around and caught a glimpse of her face. He chuckled.

"Stop looking so indignant."

"I'm not," she lied.

"Sure you are. But you're wrong."

With that he bent close, cupped her face and kissed her. She wrapped her arms around him as she surrendered to the need between them. He shifted his weight.

"Step out of the tub, Kari."

She broke the kiss long enough to see what she

was doing, then did as he requested. When he'd moved out, as well, he dragged a towel off the rack and flung it on the tile counter, then opened a drawer by the sink and pulled out a condom.

Before she knew what was going on, he'd lifted her to the counter, then dropped to his knees between her spread legs. She knew instantly what he was going to do and found herself halfway to paradise before his tongue even touched her there.

Seconds after the first intimate kiss, every muscle in her body tensed. She felt herself spiraling out of control. He brought her close to the edge, but this time instead of letting her down gently, then building her again, he stopped and stood up.

"It'll be okay," he promised, slipping on the condom.

He moved between her legs and began to kiss her neck. Shivers rippled through her as he stroked her breasts and nipples. She felt a hard probing, and instinctively she parted for him, then reached to guide him in.

This time there wasn't any pain. He still stretched her, but it didn't seem as much as it had last night. She was wet and ready, and the combination of his kissing and his fingers on her breasts made it difficult for her to think about anything but surrender.

He began to move in and out of her. With each slow thrust, she felt her body molding itself around him a little more and a little more. When he moved to kiss her mouth, she welcomed him, pulling him close. His hand dropped from her breasts to between her legs, where he rubbed against her most sensitive place, moving in counterpoint to his thrusting, bringing her closer and closer until she had no choice but to scream his name as her release claimed her.

She couldn't believe what was happening. The orgasm filled her inside and out, while he continued to move, drawing out the pleasure until he, too, stiffened and exhaled her name. They climaxed together, her body rippling around him, his surging. As the last tendrils of release drifted away, Gage raised his head and looked into her eyes.

At that moment she could see down to his soul and didn't doubt he could do the same. The profound connection shook her to the core of her being, and she knew then that nothing would ever be the same.

Still tingling from their recent encounter, Kari dressed and followed Gage down to the kitchen for breakfast. Her emotions seemed to have stabilized, but the sensation of having experienced something profound didn't go away. Still, participating in the ordinary helped. He pulled out eggs and bacon, while she grabbed bread from the freezer for toast.

Every inch of her body felt contented. The occasional aftermath of pleasure shot through her, making her catch her breath as she had a sensual flashback. Gage sure knew how to have a good time both in and out of bed, she thought happily.

"Scrambled all right?" he asked, holding up several eggs.

"Perfect. And I like my bacon extra crisp."

"That's my girl."

While she set the table, he started cooking. Soon

the scent of eggs and bacon filled the kitchen. Kari poured them more coffee, then put the toast on a plate she'd warmed in the oven. At the same time he carried two frying pans to the table and set them on the extra place mats.

They sat down across from each other, and Gage offered her the bacon. Kari liked that things were easy between them. No awkward moments, no bumping as they moved. She couldn't imagine the morning after being so comfortable with any of the other men she'd gone out with in the past few years. Of course, she doubted she would have spent the night with them, anyway.

She looked up, prepared to share her observation, when she caught Gage looking past her. The faraway look in his eyes told her that he was thinking about something other than their lovemaking. He'd remembered what he'd learned the night before. Her heart ached for him.

She sighed.

He glanced at her. "What?"

"I just wish I could find something magical to say so you'd feel better."

"Not possible."

"I know."

Everything had changed for him. In a single moment, he'd lost the anchor to his world—his past. He'd always prided himself on being one of the fifth generation of Reynolds to live in Possum Landing. He'd been his father's son. He'd—

She frowned. Why did that have to be different? "Gage, I understand that you no longer have the biological connection to Ralph Reynolds that you had before, but that doesn't mean he's not your father.''

He glared at her. ''He's not my father.''

''That's just biology. What about the heart? He still loved you from the second you were born. He held you and taught you and supported you. He came to every football and baseball game you ever played in. He taught you to fish, and drive. All those dad things.''

''How could he have loved me?'' he asked bitterly. ''His wife had cheated on him. I was another man's bastard.''

She didn't have all the answers, but she was very sure about one thing. ''No one seeing the two of you together could doubt his feelings for you. I saw it every time we went over there. His love for you lit up his whole face. You can't doubt that.''

He shrugged as if he wasn't sure he believed her. Kari didn't know how else to express her feelings. Maybe with time Gage would be able to look at the past and see his father's actions for what they were— a parent's love for his child.

But now wasn't the time to push, so she changed the subject and they discussed renovations on her grandmother's house as they finished breakfast. She'd just poured them a last cup of coffee when there was a knock on the front door.

When Gage didn't budge, she asked, ''Want me to get that?''

They both knew who it was. Edie was familiar enough with her son's schedule to know what time he had to leave for work. A quick glance at the clock told Kari there was more than an hour until he had to head out to the station.

She put down the coffeepot and walked to the front door. She had the sudden thought that it didn't look good for her to be here this early. What would Edie think? Then she reminded herself that after what had happened the previous evening, Gage's sleeping arrangements would be the last thing on his mother's mind. She pulled open the door.

"Hi, Edie," she said gently as she took in the other woman's drawn face. Edie looked older than her years, and tired, as if all the life had been sucked out of her.

Edie swallowed, then nodded without speaking. She didn't seem surprised to see Kari as she stepped into the house, but she didn't move past the foyer.

"How is he?"

"Okay, considering. A little confused and angry."

"That makes sense."

Edie wore jeans and a loose T-shirt. The clothes seemed to hang on her. Worry drew her eyebrows together.

"He's in the kitchen," Kari said at last. "I was just about to make more coffee. Do you want some?"

"No coffee for me, thanks."

Edie didn't seem startled to find Kari making coffee in her son's house, either. No doubt she wasn't thinking about something as inconsequential as that.

Impulsively Kari touched her arm. "He'll get over it," she promised. "He needs time."

"I know."

Tears filled Edie's eyes. She blinked them back, then followed Kari to the kitchen.

Gage stood at the sink, scraping dishes and loading the dishwasher. He didn't turn at the sound of their footsteps.

Great. So he was going to make this as difficult as possible for everyone.

"Gage, your mom's here."

"G-Gage?" Edie's voice shook as she spoke.

He put the last plate in the dishwasher and turned to look at her. Kari caught her breath. His face was so set, it could have been carved from stone. He looked angry and unapproachable. She wanted to run for safety, and she wasn't even the one with the recent confession. She could only imagine how Edie felt.

"You two need to talk," she said gently. "As it's a private matter, I'll head home."

Gage spared her a quick glance. "You can stay if you'd like. You already know as much as I do."

Kari shifted uncomfortably. "I know, but your mom would probably be more comfortable to keep it just family."

Edie sighed. "No, Kari. If you're willing to stay, I think you should. Gage may need to have a friend."

Kari hesitated, then nodded slowly. She wasn't sure how she would describe her relationship with Gage. *Friend* was as good a word as any. She motioned to the now cleared table, then crossed to the counter and fixed a fresh pot of coffee. Gage finished with the dishes, then moved to the table. No one spoke until Kari returned to her seat.

Talk about awkward, she thought grimly as they

sat in silence. She glanced from mother to son. Edie had pulled a tissue out of her pocket and was twisting it between her fingers.

"I know what you're thinking," she began, as the coffeemaker began to drip. "That I cheated on your father. I suppose that's technically true, but that's not the whole truth." She glanced up at her son. "I loved your father with all my heart. It started the day I met him and it's never faded. Not even once."

"Then, why the hell am I some other man's bastard?"

She flinched slightly but didn't look away. "The trouble began about a year after we married. We'd wanted a big family and had been trying from the very beginning. When nothing happened, we went to the doctor. We found out we couldn't have children."

Chapter Ten

Couldn't have children? "But you have two," Kari said before she could stop herself. She bit her lower lip. "Sorry."

Gage surprised her by reaching across the table and covering her hand with his. "It's okay."

She smiled gratefully as he turned his attention to his mother. "Are you saying Quinn and I are adopted?"

Edie shook her head. "No. We… It was difficult. Thirty years ago they couldn't do as much to help infertile couples. We each took tests and found out that Ralph was the one who couldn't have children. There was something wrong with his sperm."

"So you went out and had an affair?"

Gage's rage was a tangible presence in the room.

Edie flinched slightly and turned away, but not before Kari saw the tears return to her eyes.

Kari squeezed his fingers. "You have to listen. If you want to be angry when she's done, that's your right, but let her talk."

His jaw tightened, but he didn't release her hand or disagree. He nodded slightly, indicating his mother should go on.

Edie glanced from Kari to Gage, then continued. "As I said, there weren't as many options back then. Your father...Ralph and I didn't have a lot of money. We explored different treatments, discussed adoption. I was comfortable with that, but he didn't want to go through the process. He was concerned that we wouldn't know where the child came from or who its parents were. You know how that sort of thing was important to him."

Gage nodded curtly.

Kari ached for them both. Nothing about this was easy—she could feel their pain, understand the distance between them. Family and heritage *had* been important to Gage's father, and to Gage. So where did that leave him now? Who *were* his people? Where *was* he from?

"He kept saying he wanted me to experience having my own child. We fought and argued and cried together. At one point he threatened to leave me. But I begged him not to go. In the end, he came up with a compromise. That I would find someone who looked like him and get pregnant."

Gage's head snapped up, and he glared at his

mother. "You're telling me this was *his* idea?" His tone clearly stated he didn't believe her.

"I can't prove it," she murmured. "I can only tell you that except for this, I've never lied to you."

Kari held her breath. She believed Edie. There was too much anguish in the other woman's eyes for it to be anything but the truth. Yet Gage hesitated.

Without committing himself to accepting or not, he said, "Go on."

She hesitated a second, then continued. "We fought about that, as well," Edie said. "In the end, I agreed. I went up to Dallas because we didn't want the scandal of me being with someone from around here. Word would get out, and we didn't want anyone to know the truth. There was a convention there. Ralph had read about it and he thought that would be the perfect place. We might not get to know much about the man, but we would know something."

She picked at the place mat in front of her. "They were all in law enforcement. It was some kind of sheriff's convention. Your biological father—Earl Haynes—was a sheriff."

Kari tried to keep her face blank but doubted she succeeded. Involuntarily her gaze flew to the star on Gage's chest. He'd wanted to be a sheriff all his life— at least, that's what he'd always told her.

His fingers tightened on hers.

"So that's where you met him?" he asked coldly.

"Yes. I met him the first day. He was tall and dark haired, and very charming. We got to know each other. At first I didn't think I could go through with it, but I felt I had to. After a few days, I found myself caring for Earl in a way I hadn't thought I would.''

Gage glared at her. ''You fell for him?''

''Maybe. I don't know. I'd never been with anyone but Ralph. Earl was like him, but different, too. Exciting. He'd seen a lot of the world, been with a lot of women. I didn't know how to be intimate without giving away a piece of my heart.''

Tears trickled from the corners of her eyes. She brushed them away. ''I was so confused, and ashamed. I wanted to go home and I didn't. Earl asked me to go back to California with him, but I couldn't. I knew I belonged with Ralph, so I came home.''

Gage tore his hand free of Kari's light hold and sprang to his feet. ''Who the hell are you? How dare you come in here and tell me you didn't just sleep with some man to get pregnant, but that you also fell for him. You said you loved my father. You said you never stopped loving him.''

''I didn't,'' Edie said, pleading with her son. ''I did love him. Earl distracted me from what was important. Do you think I'm proud of what happened or how I felt? I don't want to tell you this, Gage, but I have to. You need to understand the circumstances so you'll know why things were the way they were.''

Gage crossed to the sink, where he stood with his back to the table. When he didn't say anything else, Edie went on.

''I came back home and we found out I was pregnant. Ralph never said anything about what had happened. He never asked or blamed me, and when you were born, he was as proud as any father could have been. He loved you with every fiber of his being.''

Gage visibly stiffened, but didn't speak. Edie looked at Kari, who gave her a reassuring smile.

''You also looked like Ralph, which pleased him,'' Edie said, then swallowed. ''Everything was perfect. We had you, we had each other. But I couldn't forget. What I didn't know then was that my feelings for Earl were just a girlish fantasy—the result of never having been on a date with a man other than Ralph. I mistook infatuation for love, and when you were three months old, I returned to Dallas.''

Gage swore loudly. ''You saw him again?''

Edie nodded. ''I couldn't help myself. I didn't tell Ralph. I left the baby with my mother and drove to Dallas. I only went for one night.'' She sighed heavily. ''Let's just say, I learned my lesson. I saw the difference between infatuation and real love, and I saw clearly who was the better man. I came home, but it was too late.''

Kari was stunned. Ralph must have been furious with his young wife. The first time they'd agreed on a plan. But to return to Earl Haynes again…

Gage crossed to the table and braced his hands on the back of the chair. ''Quinn,'' he breathed.

Kari stared at him. Of course. His younger brother. How could she have forgotten?

Edie nodded. ''Ralph didn't understand. He was furious and so very hurt. We nearly divorced. I still loved him with all my heart and I begged him to forgive me for being such a fool. In the end, he did forgive me. Then we found out I was pregnant. He didn't take it well.''

Gage straightened. "No wonder," he said slowly. "No wonder he hated Quinn. My brother was a constant reminder of your betrayal.''

Tears filled Edie's eyes again. "I could never convince him differently. I tried to make things right for Quinn, but I couldn't make up for his father not loving him.''

Gage stared at his mother. She'd been a part of his life for as long as he could remember, but suddenly he didn't know her. It was as if a stranger sat at the table telling him secrets from the past.

He wanted to scream out his anger. He wanted to throw something, break something, hurt something. He wanted to turn back time and forget all he'd been told so he wouldn't have to know. He wanted to put the cloth box back in the trash can and never open it.

"You lied," he said wearily. "Both of you.'' Mother and father. Except Ralph wasn't his father. He was no relation at all.

His mother, who had always known what he was thinking, stared at him. "Ralph *is* your father in every way that matters. Nothing can change that. You have a past with him and it will always be there.''

Gage shook his head. He'd had enough for one day. "I need to get to work.''

His mother wiped her face. "There's more, Gage. More things you need to hear.''

He couldn't imagine what those things might be. Nor did he want to. "Not now.''

"Then, when?''

"I don't know."

"It has to be soon."

He wanted to ask why. He wanted to refuse her request. Instead, he nodded.

She rose slowly; it seemed she'd become old overnight. After walking to the doorway, she paused as if she would say more. Then she turned and left.

Gage crossed to the window and stared out at the morning. The sky was a clear Texas blue, the temperature already in the eighties. The central air unit he'd replaced three years ago kept the house cool, as did several ceiling fans. He focused on those now, on their whisper-quiet sound and the faint brush of air against the back of his neck. He heard Kari walk up behind him. She placed a hand on the small of his back.

"Gage," she said gently.

He didn't move. "What else could she have to say?" he asked. "Think there's another bombshell?"

"I don't know."

"I don't want to hear anything else. I don't want to talk to her again."

Behind him, Kari sighed. He heard the exhale, felt her disapproval.

"I know this has been a shock, but in time you'll see—"

He spun to face her. "See what? That everything I've believed all my life is a lie? I don't want to see that. I don't want to see that my mother went off to get herself pregnant by a man she'd never met before. Or that she liked doing it with him so much, she went again the following year. I don't want to finally understand why my father always hated my brother. I don't want it to be real and not just something Quinn imagined. I don't have to know any of it.''

She stood her ground. ''There's more to it than that.''

''Is there? Like what? Am I really a part of the Reynolds family? Is Ralph really my father?''

''Of course. Yes, to both. You're furious about something that happened over thirty years ago. You're just learning it now, so it has a big impact on you, but these are not new events. Nothing has changed but your perception. You love your mom— you always have. Despite everything, I know that's not going to change. All I'm saying is that you both need time, and that you have to be careful not to say things you'll regret.''

''She's the one who should have regrets,'' he said bitterly.

''I'm sure she regrets hurting her husband, but I don't believe for a second she regrets either you or Quinn.''

He couldn't disagree with that. However, he was not in the mood to be reasonable. ''Interesting all this advice coming from you,'' he growled. ''Last I heard, you weren't so quick to forgive your family for what they did to you.''

Finally he had gotten what he'd thought he wanted. Kari dropped her gaze and took a step back. But instead of feeling vindicated, he only felt lousy.

''Sorry,'' he said quickly. ''I shouldn't have said that.''

''No, you're right. I want to say that my situation

is different, and of course it is. Every situation is different. But your point is that I'm not in a place to throw stones. I can't argue with that.''

He held out his arms and she stepped into his embrace. ''I hate this,'' he murmured into her hair. ''The information, the questions, how it's all changing.''

''I know.''

''It will never be the same again. I'm not who I was.''

''You're exactly the same man you were at this time yesterday.''

No, he wasn't. She couldn't see the changes, but he knew they were there.

''I don't belong here anymore.''

Kari raised her head and stared at him. ''Possum Landing is still your home. I'm the one who wanted to get away and see the world, but you'd already done that. You wanted to come home.''

''Is it home?'' he asked. ''There aren't five generations anymore. At least, not in my history.''

''I'm sorry,'' she whispered.

''Yeah. Me, too.''

He released her, then glanced at his watch. ''I have to get to the station. Are you going to be around tonight?''

''Sure.''

''Can I come by?''

''Absolutely.''

Gage spent the morning dealing with the crisis of two teenage boys from a neighboring town taking a joyride through a field at four in the morning. They'd been drunk and damn lucky. When they'd plowed through a barbed-wire fence and jerked loose several fence posts, the one that had shot through their front window had missed them both.

The rancher was threatening charges, while one parent thought jail time would teach his wayward son a lesson and the other kept saying "Boys will be boys."

"They'll be dead boys if they keep this up," Gage said flatly to the four adults. "I'm booking them both. They have clean records, so I doubt they'll get more than a warning and some community service. Maybe it will be enough to teach them a lesson, maybe not."

Then he stalked out before any of the parents could speak with him. Normally he didn't mind taking the time to deal individually with kids headed in the wrong direction. He liked to think that he'd steered more than one teenager back onto the straight and narrow. But not today. Today all he could think about was the lie that was his past, and his suddenly unclear future.

He stalked into his office and closed the door. Several staff members looked up at the sound. Gage couldn't remember the last time he'd shut himself off from what was going on in the station. Mostly he liked to be in the thick of things. Hell, maybe he should have just stayed home.

But instead of clocking out for the day, he reached for the phone and dialed a number from memory. He gave the appropriate name, number and password to the computer before a pleasant-sounding woman picked up the phone.

"Bailey," she said crisply.

"I'd like to get a message to my brother," he said.

He heard her typing on a keyboard. "Yes, Sheriff Reynolds. I have authorization right here. What is the message?"

There was the rub, he thought grimly. What to say? "Tell him…" He cleared his throat. "Tell him to call me as soon as he can. It's a family matter. No one's sick or anything," he added quickly.

"Very well, sir. I'll see that he gets the message."

Gage didn't bother asking when that might happen. He'd tried to contact Quinn enough to know it could be weeks before he heard back, maybe even a couple of months. Or it could be tomorrow. There was no way to be sure.

"Thanks," he said, and hung up.

He leaned back in his chair and stared into the office. Instead of seeing people working, talking and carrying files, he saw his past. The idyllic days of growing up in Possum Landing. He'd been so damn sure he belonged. Now he wasn't sure of anything. His identity had been ripped from him.

As far as he could tell, the only good thing to come out of all of this was an explanation for his brother. Not that an answer would be enough to make up for Quinn's particular hell while he'd been growing up.

Gage had never understood the problem between father and son. Gage could do no wrong and Quinn could do no right. Ralph hadn't cared about his younger son's good grades, ability at sports or school awards. The only time he'd bothered to attend a game of Quinn's was when Gage was on the same team.

He'd never said a word when Quinn made the varsity baseball team during his sophomore year. Quinn had been a ghost in the house, and now he lived his life like a demon. All the pain, and for what? A lie?

Gage turned in his chair and gazed at the computer. The blinking cursor seemed to taunt him. *Lies,* it blinked over and over. *Lies, lies, lies.*

So what was the truth?

There was only one way to find out. He clicked on a law-enforcement search engine, then typed in a single name: Earl Haynes.

The ancient, shuddering air-conditioning didn't come close to cooling the attic. Unable to face more painting because it reminded her of Gage, Kari had decided on cleaning out the attic, instead. She'd opened all the windows and had dragged up a floor fan that she'd set on high. It might be hot up here, but at least there was a breeze.

She sat on the dusty floor in front of several open boxes and trunks. Grammy had kept everything. Clothes, hats, shoes, pictures, newspapers, magazines, blankets, lamps. Kari shook her head as she gazed at the collection of about a dozen old, broken lamps. Some were lovely and probably worth repairing, but others were just plain old and ugly. They should have been thrown out years ago.

But that wasn't her grandmother's way, she thought as she dug into the next layer of the trunk in front of her. She encountered something soft, like fur, then something hard like—

"Whoa!"

She jumped to her feet, prepared to flee. There was an animal in there.

An old umbrella lay by the door. She picked it up and cautiously approached the trunk. A couple of good, hard pokes didn't produce any movement. Kari used the umbrella to push aside several garments, then stared down at an unblinking black eye.

"Well, that's totally gross," she said, bending over and picking up a fox stole with the fox head and tail still attached. "All you need are your little feet, huh?"

While she wasn't one to turn down a nicely cooked steak, she drew the line at wearing an animal head across her shoulders. This poor creature was going right into the give-away pile.

The next box held more contemporary items, including some baby and toddler clothes that had probably belonged to her. She held up a ruffly dress, trying to remember when she'd ever been that small.

"Not possible," she murmured.

Below that was her uniform from her lone year as a cheerleader, back in middle school, and below that was something white and sparkly.

Her breath caught in her throat as she pulled out the long, flowing strapless gown. The fabric of the bodice twisted once in front, then wrapped around to the back. Clinging fabric fell all the way to the floor. She crossed to the old mirror in the corner and held the dress up in front of her.

She'd never actually worn it, but she'd tried it on about four hundred times. Her prom dress. Kari squeezed her eyes shut for a second, then stared at her reflection. If she squinted, she didn't look all that different. With a little pretending, it could be eight years ago, when she'd been so young and innocent and in love, and Gage had been the man of her dreams.

Gage. She sighed. She'd been trying *not* to think about him all day. That was the point of keeping busy, because if she wasn't, she worried and fretted, neither of which were productive. Unfortunately, the blast from the past in her arms had dissolved her mature resolve to keep an emotional distance from the situation.

Instead, she remembered her excitement at the thought of going to her prom with Gage. After all, the other girls were going with boys from school, or from one of the nearby colleges. But she had been going with a *man.*

Only, that hadn't happened. Instead of dancing the night away, she'd been on a bus heading to New York. Instead of laughing, she'd spent the night in tears. And while she couldn't regret the outcome— leaving had been the right thing to do—she was ashamed of how she'd handled the situation.

"Too young," she told her reflection. "Of course, if I was old enough to be in love with Gage, I was old enough to tell him I was leaving, right?"

Her reflection didn't answer.

She put the dress down and walked to the stairs. She wanted to call Gage and ask if he was all right. She wanted to go to the station and see him. But she couldn't. Not today. Yesterday all those things would have been fine because he wouldn't have misunderstood her motives, but now everything was different. Now he might think she was pressuring him because of last night and this morning. She didn't want him thinking she was one of those clingy women who gave their hearts every time they made love with a man. She wasn't like that at all. At least, she didn't think she was. Not that she had any experience in that particular arena.

No, the reason she wanted to talk to Gage had nothing to do with their intimacy and everything to do with what he'd just found out. She was being a good friend, nothing more.

The phone rang, interrupting her thoughts. She dashed down the narrow attic stairs and flew toward her grandmother's bedroom, where the upstairs phone was kept.

"Hello?" she said breathlessly. Gage had called. He'd called!

"Ms. Asbury?" a cool, female voice asked.

Kari's heart sank. "Yes."

"I'm Mrs. Wilson. I'm calling you about your résumé. Do you have a moment?"

"Sure." Kari sat on the bed and tried to catch her breath.

Fifteen minutes later she had an interview scheduled for the following week. At this rate she would have a job in no time, she told herself as she hung up. In Abilene or Dallas or some other Texas city.

Just not Possum Landing.

Kari didn't know where that thought had come from, but she didn't like it. She was back in town for a visit, she reminded herself. This time was about fixing up the house to sell it, not reconnecting with anyone. This wasn't about Gage.

She repeated that thought forcefully, as if the energy invoked would make it more convincing. Unfortunately, all the energy in the world didn't change the fact that she had a bad feeling she was lying to herself.

Chapter Eleven

Gage showed up at Kari's door at a little after six. Until he'd walked from his house to hers, he hadn't been sure he would come. He'd nearly canceled a dozen times, reaching for the phone to call and tell her that something had come up. Or that he needed to spend the night by himself to figure out what he was going to do next. This wasn't her problem; she didn't need to be involved.

But every time he picked up the phone, he put it back down again. Maybe he *should* spend the evening thinking by himself, but he couldn't. Not yet. In the past twenty-four hours, he'd come to need Kari. He needed to see her, to be with her, to hear her voice and hold her close. He didn't know what the needing meant and he wasn't sure he liked it. But he acknowledged it.

Kari was a part of his past. Expecting anything more than a few nostalgic conversations and maybe a couple of tumbles in bed was a mistake. *More* than a mistake—hadn't he already fallen for her once?

So here he stood on her front porch, needing to see her and hating the need. He reached out and knocked once.

When she opened the front door and smiled at him, he felt as if things weren't as bad as he'd first thought.

"I come bearing gifts," he said, handing her a bucket of fried chicken with all the fixings that he'd picked up on the way home. "The diner still makes the best anywhere."

Kari laughed and took the container. Her blond hair swayed slightly as she shook her head. "Do you know, I haven't had fried chicken since I left here eight years ago?"

"Then, I would say it's about time."

She inhaled deeply, then licked her lips. "I guess so."

Still smiling, she stepped back to let him in the house. He walked inside, a folder still tucked under one arm.

"What's that?" she asked.

"Information on my biological father," he said. "I did some research today. I'll fill you in over dinner."

She led him into the kitchen. The small table by the window had been set for two. She offered wine or beer—he took the latter.

He watched her as she crossed to the refrigerator and pulled out a bottle. She wore a loose sundress that skimmed her curves before flaring out slightly at the hem. Her feet were bare. He could see that she'd painted her toenails a light pink. Gold hoops glinted at her ears, while makeup emphasized the perfect bone structure of her face.

When she was younger, he'd thought she was the prettiest girl he'd ever seen. Sometimes when they'd gone out he hadn't wanted to do anything more than sit across from her and gaze at her face.

Time had changed her. The twenty or so pounds she'd lost had angled her face and hollowed her cheeks. She'd been a pretty girl before and now she was a beautiful woman. He could imagine her in twenty years…still amazing.

She raised her eyebrows. ''Is there a sudden wart on my nose?''

''No. I was thinking how nice you look.''

She glanced down at the dress. ''I'd say something like 'this old thing,' but it happens to be from an exclusive designer's summer collection. He offered it to me as a going-away present when I was in his show right before I left.''

''It's nice.''

''It retails for about two thousand dollars.''

Gage nearly spit. ''You're kidding.''

''Not even a little.'' She grinned. ''Suddenly I look a little better than nice, huh?''

''You always do, and it has nothing to do with the dress.''

She sighed. ''Nice line. Perfect timing, very sincere. You've gotten better, Gage, and I wouldn't have thought that was possible.''

He shrugged off the compliment. He hadn't meant

his comment as a line—he'd been telling the truth. But explaining that would take them in a difficult direction. Better to change the subject.

"Are you telling the truth when you say you haven't had fried chicken since you left?"

"Of course." She carried the large bucket to the table and pulled off the top. "I haven't had anything fried. It's not easy staying as thin as I've been. No fried chicken, no French fries, no burgers." She tilted her head. "I've had ice cream a couple of times and chocolate. I let myself have one small piece once a month. Now that I'm a normal person again, I can eat what I want."

"Then, let's get started," he said, putting his folder on the counter and joining her at the table.

Fifteen minutes later, they were up to their elbows in fried chicken, mashed potatoes and coleslaw. Kari licked her fingers and sighed. "I'd forgotten how good this is. Even Grammy couldn't come close to the recipe."

"It's been passed down for several generations. You have the same chance of getting the family recipe out of Mary Ellen as you have of stopping the rotation of the earth. Many folks have tried over the years. There was even a break-in once. Only the recipe book was taken."

"You're kidding."

"Nope. We never did find out who'd done it. Of course, Mary Ellen told everyone who would listen that the fried chicken recipe had been given to her by her mama and no one in the family was ever fool enough to write it down."

Kari laughed.

Gage smiled slightly, but his humor faded. Talk of things being passed down reminded him of his own situation.

She read his mind. "What did you find out today?"

He wiped his hands on a napkin, then reached for the folder he'd left on the counter. After flipping it open, he read the computer printout.

"Earl Haynes is from a small town in Northern California. Like my mom said, he's a sheriff, or at least he was. He's down in Florida now. Retired and living with a woman young enough to be his daughter."

He flipped the page. "He had four sons by his first marriage, and a daughter by another woman. Apparently old Earl likes getting women pregnant, even if he doesn't like sticking around."

"Isn't it a little early to be judging him so harshly? You don't know all the circumstances."

He shrugged. There was no point in explaining that he had a knot in his gut warning him the information about his father wasn't going to be good.

"Let's just say the first reports aren't that impressive," he told her.

"It's interesting that he's a sheriff," she said. "You went into law enforcement and Quinn went into the military. I wonder if that's significant."

He didn't want it to be. The little he'd learned about Earl Haynes told him that he didn't want the man to matter at all.

"What about your brothers?" she asked when he didn't say anything.

He looked at her. ''What do you mean?''

''You said Earl Haynes had four sons and a daughter. So you have five half siblings. Four of them are brothers.''

Gage hadn't thought of that. He'd always regretted that both his parents were only children—there hadn't been any cousins. Now he suddenly had brothers and a sister.

''Well, hell,'' he muttered.

''Do you want to get in touch with them?''

''I don't know.''

He hadn't thought that far ahead. He didn't want to have any part of Earl Haynes or his family.

''Let's talk about something else,'' he said. ''Tell me about your day.''

Kari took a bite of mashed potatoes. When she swallowed, she glanced at him from under her lashes. ''I didn't get any painting done,'' she admitted. ''I was too restless. I went upstairs and started cleaning the attic.''

''Must have been hot.''

She grinned. ''It was. Even with all the windows open and a fan going. I found some interesting stuff, though. Old clothes, some jewelry.''

She hesitated, then sighed. ''Grammy kept a lot of my old clothes and toys. I was feeling very nostalgic.''

''What did you see there?''

''My old prom dress. I can't remember how many times I tried it on. I used to put my hair in different styles, then try on the dress to see what looked the best. I wanted everything about that night to be perfect.''

Only, it hadn't been, he thought sadly. She'd disappeared and he'd been left holding a diamond engagement ring.

''I'm sorry, Gage,'' she said softly. ''Sorry for running off, sorry for not telling you what I was so afraid of. Mostly I'm sorry for hurting you and leaving you to clean up my mess.''

The words had come years too late, but it was good to hear them. ''You don't have to apologize. I know you didn't take off just to hurt me.''

''I should have said something. I was just so scared.''

''You had a right to be.'' For the first time he could admit the truth. ''You were too young. Hell, I was too young. I'd been so sure about what I wanted that I didn't want to think there might be another side.''

Kari leaned back in her chair and voiced the question she'd asked herself over the years. ''I wonder if we would have made it.''

''I don't know. I like to think we would have.''

''Me, too.''

Kari studied him—his dark eyes, the firm set of his jaw. Tonight his mouth was set...no smile teased at the corner. He participated in the conversation, but she could tell that he was distracted.

Seeing him like this was such a change. The Gage she remembered had always known his place in the world. While the man before her now was still capable and confident, his foundation had shifted. She wondered how he would be affected.

His pain and confusion were tangible. Impulsively, she stretched her hand across the small table and touched his arm. "Tell me what I can do to help," she said.

"Nothing." He shrugged. "I don't think I'm going to be good company tonight."

The statement surprised her. "I'm not expecting a comedy show," she said lightly. "I thought—"

She didn't want to say what she'd thought. That he would stay with her tonight. That they would make love in her small bed, then curl up together and sleep in a tangle of arms and legs. Even if they weren't intimate, she wanted to be physically close. But Gage was already getting to his feet.

"I'm sorry," he said. "I've got a lot to think about. Maybe we can try this in a couple of days if I can take a rain check?"

As he was already standing, she didn't seem to have much choice. "Sure. I understand."

And she did. The problem was, she was also disappointed.

He started to collect plates, but she shooed him away. "You brought dinner," she protested. "I can handle cleanup."

He nodded and headed for the door. She followed him.

He paused long enough to drop a quick kiss on her forehead and offer a promise to be in touch. Then he was gone. Kari was left standing by herself, wondering what had gone wrong.

Despite the warmth of the evening, a coldness crept through her. They'd made love the previous night and this morning, but tonight Gage hadn't wanted to stay. Their intimacy obviously hadn't touched him the same way it had touched her. He'd been able to withdraw and regroup, while she'd…

Kari wasn't sure what had happened to her. How much of what was happening was due to her personal insecurities and how much of it was Gage withdrawing? Was he really going to a place where she wouldn't be able to reach him?

She hated the anxiousness that filled her, and the restlessness. She wanted to be with him. Obviously, she'd connected more when they'd made love than she'd realized.

That's all it was, she told herself as she returned to the kitchen. An emotional reaction to a physical encounter. There was no way she was foolish enough to let her heart get engaged. She'd already fallen in love with Gage once. That had ended badly. She was smart enough not to make the same mistake again.

Wasn't she?

Kari had barely finished dressing the following morning when there was a loud knocking on her front door. Her heart jumped in her chest as she hurried down the stairs.

Gage, she thought happily, her bare feet moving swiftly as she unfastened the lock and turned the knob.

But the person standing in front of her wasn't a tall, handsome, dark-haired man. Instead, a stylishly dressed woman in her forties smiled at Kari.

"Hello, darling," her mother said. "I know I

should have called and warned you I was stopping by, but the decision to come was an impulse. Your father and I are going to London in the morning. I wanted to come see my baby girl before we left.''

''Hi, Mom,'' Kari said, trying to summon enthusiasm as she stepped back to let her mother into the house.

Aurora presented her cheek for a kiss. Kari responded dutifully, then offered coffee.

''I would love some,'' her mother said. ''I was up before dawn so I could make the drive here.''

''You drove?'' Kari asked in some surprise.

''I thought about flying into Dallas and then driving down, but by the time I got to the airport, waited for my flight, then rented a car, it seemed to take as much time.''

She smiled as she spoke. Aurora Reynolds was a beautiful woman. She'd made it to the final five of a state beauty pageant during her senior year of high school before abandoning her plans of fame and fortune to marry an up-and-coming engineer. Like her mother before her, and her mother's mother before that, she'd married at eighteen, had her first child by the time she was nineteen and had never worked outside the home a day in her life.

''I think I remember where everything is,'' Aurora said as she bustled around the kitchen. She spooned grounds into the coffeemaker, then retrieved bread from the freezer and pulled the toaster from its place under the counter.

As she worked, she chattered, bringing Kari up to date on the various events in everyone's life.

"I don't understand why he married her," she was saying. "Your brother is the most stubborn man. I said twenty-three was too young—but did he listen? Of course not."

Kari nodded without actually participating. She was used to fleeting visits during which her mother would drop in, talk for hours about people she didn't know, air-kiss and then take off for some exotic destination. The pattern had been repeating itself for as long as she could remember.

As to her mother's comment about her "knowing" anything about her brothers, Kari didn't. She saw them once every couple of years for a day or so. Theirs wasn't a close family. At least, not for her. She couldn't say what the four of them did when she wasn't around. For all she knew, they lived in each other's pockets.

"How are you progressing with the sorting?" her mother asked after she put bread in the toaster and there was nothing to do but wait.

"It's slow but interesting. Grammy kept so much. I found a fox stole yesterday. It nearly scared the life out of me."

Aurora laughed. "I remember that old thing. I used to play dress-up with it."

"Would you like to have it?" Kari had planned to give the thing away, but if her mother wanted it, she could have it.

"No, darling. I prefer the memory to the dusty reality."

She leaned against the counter, a tall, blond beauty who still turned heads. Looking fresh and stylish in cotton trousers and a crisp blouse, she seemed to defy the heat. Kari knew what small success she'd had as a model came from her mother's side of the family.

"There are some old dresses and other things," Kari persisted. "Do you want to look at any of them?"

"I don't think so. I didn't inherit my mother's desire to save everything. But if there are some photo albums, I'll take a look at them."

"Sure." Kari was eager to escape the kitchen. "Dozens. I have a few in the living room. Let me get them."

She hurried into the other room and grabbed an armful of photo albums covering events over the past fifty years.

"I think your high school pictures are in this one," Kari said, setting the stack on the counter and picking up the top album.

"Hmm." Her mother didn't sound very interested as she poured them each coffee and carried the mugs to the table. Several slices of toast already sat on a plate there.

Her mother put down the mugs, then sorted through the albums. She came across one filled with pictures of Kari from about age three to eight or nine.

"What a sweet girl you were," her mother said with a sigh. "You hair was so light, and look at that smile."

Aurora's expression softened as she slowly turned pages. Kari watched her in some surprise. Her mother hadn't bothered to keep her around all those years ago, so why was she going misty over a few pictures?

She didn't voice the question, but her mother must have known what she was thinking because she closed the album and stared at her daughter.

"You think I'm a fraud," her mother said flatly.

Kari took a step back. "No. Of course not."

"I suppose it's not a big stretch for you to assume that I never cared, but you're wrong."

Clutching the album to her chest, her mother crossed to the table and took a seat. "I remember when you left for New York. Mama was concerned because you had no one there to help you. She was afraid you'd be too stubborn to come home if things got bad, but I knew you'd be all right."

Her mother sighed, tracing her fingers along the top of the album. "I like to think you got your strength from me. That ability to do what's right even when it hurts. Leaving Gage behind wasn't easy, but it was the right thing to do, wasn't it?"

Kari sat in the chair across from her mother and nodded.

"I thought so. I've made tough decisions, too." Aurora looked past her daughter and stared out the kitchen window.

"You were such a tiny thing when you were born," she said quietly. "We had a big problem with colic and you had recurring ear infections. The doctor said you'd outgrow the problem and be fine, but in the meantime your father had been offered a job in Thailand. We talked about me staying with you because you couldn't possibly make the trip. I was terrified to be that far from a familiar doctor."

Kari tried to remember if she'd heard this story

before. From her earliest memories, she'd been in Texas and her parents had been somewhere else. Once, she'd asked to go with them when they'd come to visit. Her mother had said that was fine, but Grammy was too old to travel that far and live in a foreign country. Given the choice between her beloved Grammy and parents who were strangers, she'd chosen to stay.

"I didn't know what to do. You needed me, your father needed me. Then Mama said she would keep you for a few weeks, until things settled down. The doctor was sure you would be ready by the time you were seven or eight months old. It broke my heart to leave you, but in the end, that's what I did."

Aurora sipped her coffee, then opened the album on the table. As she turned pages, she spoke. "Once we were settled in Thailand, we found out travel wasn't as simple as we had thought. Your ear infections continued longer than we expected they would. There wasn't a doctor nearby, so I waited to bring you to join us. Then I became pregnant with your brother." She glanced up and smiled sheepishly. "That wasn't planned, I can assure you." Her smile faded and suddenly she looked every one of her years.

"I didn't want to travel the first few months. Then a wonderful doctor settled in our area. The timing was perfect, I thought. He would deliver my next child and then I could come and bring you home. I waited until your brother was three months old and then I returned here, to Possum Landing."

Her mother turned away and drew in a deep breath. "I'd been gone too long. When I finally arrived, you were nearly two and a half. I walked in the door and called your name. But you didn't remember me. You hid, and when I tried to pick you up, you cried and only Mama could calm you down.''

Kari felt her throat getting a little tight. Nothing in her mother's story was familiar, yet she sensed every word was true. Against her will, she imagined her mother's pain and heartbreak at being a stranger to her firstborn child.

''I didn't know what to do,'' Aurora said. ''I stayed for two weeks, but the situation didn't improve. I think you somehow knew that my plan was to take you away. You wouldn't let Mama out of your sight and continued to run from me. Mama wanted to keep you. She loved you as if you were her own. I couldn't fight the two of you. In the end it seemed kinder to leave you here. So I went back to Thailand without you.''

Kari nodded but found she couldn't speak. Not without tears threatening. She'd always felt she'd been abandoned by her parents, but maybe the truth wasn't so simple.

''Looking back, I can't help thinking I took the easy way out,'' her mother admitted. ''I could have dragged you with me. In time you would have accepted me as your mother. Maybe that would have been better. But I didn't. I can't say Mama didn't love you with all her heart, or raise you perfectly, but I regret what I lost. I never should have left you behind in the first place. I should have found another way.'' She offered a sad smile. ''I suppose that sounds selfish.''

"No," Kari managed to reply. "I understand." She did…sort of. Her head spun. Too much had happened too quickly. She'd come back to Possum Landing expecting to spend a few weeks fixing up her late grandmother's house. Instead, she'd come face-to-face with ghosts from her past. First Gage and now her mother.

"Now I suppose it's too late for things to be different between us," Aurora said casually, not quite meeting her daughter's eyes.

Kari hesitated. "I appreciate hearing about what really happened. It's different from what I imagined." She grabbed her coffee mug but didn't pick it up. "Why now?" she asked.

"The time was never right," her mother said. "At first, I didn't want to take you away from Mama. I always hoped…" She shrugged. "I thought you might come ask me on your own. Eventually, I realized you thought I'd simply turned my back on you."

Kari didn't respond. That had been what she'd thought. Apparently, she'd been wrong.

She thought about what she and Gage had spoken about just yesterday, when she'd told him he would have to forgive his parents if he wanted to make peace with the past. Could she do any less?

"I need some time," Kari told her mother. "This is a lot to absorb."

"That's fine." Her mother glanced at her watch. "Oh dear. I have to head back. There are a thousand and one things to do before we head to London tomorrow."

Aurora rose and Kari did the same. "Do you mind

if I keep this?'' her mother asked, motioning to the photo album.

"Take as many as you'd like. There are plenty."

Her mother smiled. "I just want this one of you."

Kari didn't know what to say, so she gave in to impulse and moved close for a hug. After Aurora disappeared in a cloud of perfume and a promise to "bring you something wonderful from London," Kari returned to the kitchen, where she poured out her now cold coffee.

Just two hours before, her world had been only mildly confusing. Now it was like living inside a tornado where everything was spinning too fast to allow her to hold on.

She didn't know what to make of her mother's story. It shouldn't change anything but her perception of the past, yet somehow everything looked different. Now she had a more clear understanding of what Gage was going through, albeit on a smaller scale.

Nothing was ever simple, she thought, moving to the side window and staring at his house. So much had happened in such a short period of time.

Chapter Twelve

Kari decided the best antidote for feeling unsettled was hard work. She finished painting the second upstairs bedroom, then started on her grandmother's room. The old pieces of furniture slid away from the walls more easily than she had anticipated. She pushed everything toward the center of the room to give herself space to work. She took down drapes, picked up throw rugs and draped drop cloths over everything. By two-thirty she was sweaty, exhausted and in need of a break.

In an effort to get away from her own company, she decided on a trip to the grocery store. As much as she might want to see Gage that night, she figured it was unlikely. So she settled on "chick" food for dinner. A salad, yummy bread, with a pint of her favorite ice cream for dessert.

She'd just stopped by the tomato display to pick out a couple for her salad when something slammed into her grocery cart. One of the wheels rolled into her foot, making her jump. Kari turned in surprise— then wished she hadn't.

Daisy stood behind her own cart, glaring at Kari. "I can't believe it," the petite redhead said, her eyes flashing with rage. "I told you about my plans for Gage, but you didn't care. Well, fine. Try for him if you want, but you're destined to fail. I might have felt sorry for you before, but now I figure you've earned it."

Kari had the urge to tilt her head and wiggle her earlobe. She couldn't have heard any of that correctly.

"I have no idea what you're talking about," she said at last.

Daisy looked disbelieving. "Sure you don't. I told you I was interested in Gage, but you didn't care. You just waltzed into his bed without giving a damn about anyone else. I'll have you know, Gage doesn't like his women that easy. But I guess you already knew that."

Kari opened her mouth, but before she could speak, Daisy narrowed her gaze.

"Don't try to deny it. I saw you leaving his place a couple of mornings ago. I doubt you'd just dropped by to borrow some coffee."

The joys of small towns, Kari thought, trying to find the humor in the situation. She shook her head. "First of all, what I do or don't do with Gage isn't anyone's business but ours. Second, I don't know why you're so put out. You and I aren't friends. In fact, we've barely met. I don't owe you anything. If you were in love with him, I might give your feelings some consideration, but you've already admitted you're not. Your interest in Gage comes from the fact that you think he'll be a good husband and father. While I'm sure he'd appreciate the endorsement, I suspect if he does decide to marry, he's going to want his future wife to be madly in love with him.''

Daisy's eyes flashed with temper. ''I suspect what he'll want is someone who doesn't take off at the first sign of trouble.''

Kari acknowledged the direct hit with a slight wince, but didn't otherwise respond to that comment. ''If Gage is interested in you,'' she said, instead, ''no one else would matter to him, so I wouldn't be a threat to you. If he's not interested, then warning me off doesn't make any difference at all.''

''You're judging me.'' Daisy was fuming. ''But you're no better. You had him and you let him go. How smart was that?''

''I was young and foolish,'' Kari admitted. ''I didn't realize how wonderful he was, but I do now.''

''You're not going to get him back.''

Kari grabbed a tomato and put it in her cart. ''I don't think you get to decide that,'' she said coolly, then pulled her cart from Daisy's and stalked away.

As she walked, she kept her head high, but she was shaking inside. The encounter had rattled her more than she wanted to admit.

As she approached the checkout stand, she thought of half a dozen things she should have said to Daisy, including the fact that at least she'd been smart enough to fall in love with him eight years ago. If Kari thought for a second that she was going to stay around and that he was interested, she would—

Kari cut that thought off before she could finish it. Being annoyed with Daisy was one thing, but acting foolishly was another. She didn't love Gage. She refused to believe she was the kind of woman who would still be in love with him after all this time. She wasn't. She hadn't secretly been waiting to come back to him. The idea was laughable.

No. She had left and she had gotten on with her life. She was still getting on with it. Gage was just a memory. The past, not the future.

Gage pulled into the cemetery and parked by the curb. He waited a long time before getting out of his car. The rational side of him knew that there was no hope of getting answers here. His father had long since moved beyond speaking.

His father.

Just thinking the words propelled him from the car. Ralph Reynolds—the name on Gage's birth certificate. The man who had loved him and raised him and shown him right from wrong. Ralph? No, he thought as he crossed the freshly cut lawn. Not Ralph. *Dad.*

Kari was right. Biology be damned. This man he had loved and mourned was his real father. He might not share the blood that ran in Gage's veins, but he had influenced him and molded him.

He crossed to the simple marble marker. Ralph Emerson Reynolds. There were the dates of his birth and death, followed by "Beloved husband and father."

He *had* been beloved, Gage reminded himself. Ralph's unexpected death from a heart attack had devastated the family. Even Quinn had been caught by surprise.

Gage crouched by the marble marker. "Hey, Dad," he said, then stopped because talking to himself in the middle of a cemetery felt strange. Then he continued. "Mama told me. About my biological father." He swallowed. "I wish you'd told me the truth. It wouldn't have changed anything."

He stared at the marble. "Okay. It would have changed things. But hearing it from you would have been better than finding out the way I did. You could have explained things to me. You could have told Quinn why he was never good enough."

Gage stood and paced on the grass. Quinn had deserved to know why his best had never mattered. Ralph Reynolds had been a great father to Gage, but he'd been a real bastard to Quinn.

"You shouldn't have done it," Gage said, spinning back to the tombstone. "You should have treated us the same. If you could accept me—someone else's son—you should have accepted him."

He wanted to rage against his father, but it was years too late. Maybe that's why he hadn't been told. Maybe Ralph had pretended; maybe he'd forgotten the truth. At least for Gage.

Damn. There weren't going to be any sudden illuminations that would set his world to rights.

His chest tightened, his throat burned. He looked

up at the sky, then back at the grave. "I still would have loved you, no matter what. Why didn't you believe that?"

There was only silence, punctuated by the background songs of the birds. There were no answers here, there was no peace. His father had long since left for another place. This problem was for the living. Which meant Gage had another stop to make.

In the way that mothers always seem to know what their sons are up to, Edie stood on the porch, watching for him as he drove up. She didn't walk down the stairs to greet him or smile. She stayed where she was, waiting to see his reaction.

He tried to remember how their last conversation had ended, but it was all a blur. Too much emotion, he thought. Too many revelations.

"Hey," he said as he climbed the stairs. He saw the front door was open and that John hovered in the front room.

"Gage."

Edie pressed her hands together. All the energy seemed to have been drained out of her. Her eyes remained dull and flat.

Without saying anything, he crossed to her and pulled her into his arms. She collapsed against him, a sudden sob catching in her throat.

"It's okay, Mama," he said, as she started to cry. "I was really pissed off, but it's okay now."

"I'm sorry," she said shakily. "So sorry. I never meant to hurt you. There were so many times I wanted to tell you the truth."

"I know." He stroked her hair. "I believe you. Dad wouldn't have wanted you to say anything. If he couldn't fix the problem, he pretended it didn't exist. Didn't we used to joke about that?"

She raised her head and stared at him. Tears dampened her cheeks. "He *is* your father, Gage. No matter what, that hasn't changed."

"I know. I lost it for a while, but it's back."

John came out and joined him. He put an arm around Edie and held out his hand to Gage. They shook, then John nodded.

"I told her you'd come around."

"Thanks."

His mother beamed at him. "Do you want to come in? We could talk. There are still some things—"

He cut her off with a quick smile. "I need some time, okay?"

He saw that she didn't want to put off the rest of whatever it was she had to share, but he didn't care if he never knew any more.

"Just a couple of days," he promised, and turned back to his car.

She and John stood on the porch, watching him as he pulled out. He waved and his mother smiled at him.

She thought everything was all right now. That it was all behind them, Gage thought as he headed back to the station. What she'd done…well, she'd had her reasons. Some he agreed with, some he didn't. It would take a long time for him to get over the fact that his mother had thought she was in love with someone else while she was still married to his father.

But what Edie and Ralph Reynolds had done…had survived…wasn't his business. He had to deal with what had had an impact on him.

The truth was that forgiving his mother and making peace with his father didn't change one fact: he was not the man he'd always thought he was.

Kari washed brushes in the sink in the utility room. It was after nine in the evening, and she focused on the task at hand in an effort to keep her brain from repeating the same thought over and over again.

It had been nearly a week since she'd seen Gage.

A week! Six days and twenty-two hours.

Why? She knew that he'd been avoiding her, but couldn't quite pin down the reason. She wanted to believe it was all about his past, but she had a bad feeling that some of it was personal. With everything else going on in his life, the last thing he would want to worry about was her virginity, or how he'd made that disappear. No doubt he thought she would already be picking out china patterns, while he'd simply been interested in getting laid.

Kari turned off the water and sighed. Okay, that was a slight exaggeration. Gage wasn't the kind of guy to only want sex for sex's sake. If he was, he would never have been so careful while they were dating. He would have pushed her, and, as much as she'd been in love with him, she would have given in.

So Gage hadn't been looking for an easy score and she wasn't looking to get married to the first man she slept with. Reality lay somewhere in between.

She set the wet brushes on a rack, then washed her hands and dried them on a towel. Despite the pulsing urge inside her, she was *not* going to cross to the front window and stare out from an opening in the lace curtains. Spying on Gage, watching for when he got home, was way too pathetic. Besides, she'd been doing it too much lately. If she wanted to talk to him, she should simply call, like a normal person. Or go to his house, or even his office. If she didn't...

Kari walked into the kitchen and crossed to the refrigerator. She'd bought a pint of cookie-dough ice cream on her last visit to the grocery, and this seemed like a fine time to have it for dinner. Despite all her logical conversations with herself, the bottom line was that she was alone on a Saturday night, watching for the boy next door to come home and ask her out. This was worse than when she was in high school. She had managed to live in a big city for eight years, have different experiences, even have something close to a successful modeling career. Yet nothing had changed. The situation would be pretty funny if it were happening to someone else.

The phone rang, causing her to slam the freezer door. Her heart rate increased. There were only two types of calls in her current world—Gage, or not Gage. This increased the pathetic factor, but was completely true.

"Hello?" she said, trying not to sound breathless.

"Hi, Kari," Gage said. "What's going on?"

Over the past week, she'd planned her conversation with him dozens of times. She'd had witty lines and blasé lines and casual questions all lined up. Now, of course, she couldn't think of anything but "Not much. I've been working on the house. Just finished painting for the day."

"I've been meaning to get back there and help you."

The road to hell and all that, she thought. "My remodeling job isn't your responsibility," she said. "How are you doing?"

"Okay. Still trying to figure things out."

Silence. She sighed. Things had been so much easier before. Before they'd made love. Before he'd found out about his past.

He cleared his throat. "The reason I phoned is that there's a big dance up at the country club. I've had a few calls from worried parents. They're concerned that the kids might be renting hotel rooms for the night. I did some checking around and it looks like a group of them are planning to spend the night at the Possum Landing Lodge. I'm on my way over to break things up. I was hoping you'd come with me."

She frowned. "To break up a party?"

"Yeah, well, the odds are that some of these teenagers are going to be going at it in the room, and I don't want to have to deal with a bunch of half-dressed girls."

Not exactly the invitation she'd been waiting for, but it was better than nothing. "Sure, I'll help."

"Great. I'll be by in about ten minutes."

"Okay. 'Bye."

She hung up, then flew upstairs to replace her paint-spattered shorts and T-shirt with a crisp summer dress. There wasn't time for a shower or a fabulous hairstyle, so she ran a brush through her hair, fluffing up the ends while she worked. After racing into the bathroom, she brushed her teeth, applied mascara and lip gloss and slipped on some silver hoops. A pair of sandals completed her outfit. She hurried back downstairs and collected her house key, then walked to the front door. She'd just reached it when Gage knocked.

She opened the door and tried not to smile at him. Against her will, her mouth curved up and every cell in her body danced. Talk about betrayal.

Even more frustrating, he looked really, really good. There were shadows under his eyes as if he hadn't been sleeping much, and his uniform was a little rumpled—but none of that mattered. Not when she could see into his eyes and watch him smile back at her.

"Hi," he said. "Thanks for the help."

"No problem."

He didn't move back, so she couldn't step out of the house. They looked at each other. He reached out his hand and lightly touched her cheek.

"I've been avoiding you."

The admission surprised her. She decided to offer one of her own. "I noticed."

"It wasn't because of…" He paused. "I've had a lot on my mind. I didn't want to dump it all on you."

"We're friends, Gage. I'm happy to listen."

"I may take you up on that. I've been doing a lot of thinking and I don't seem to be making any progress."

"Have you talked with your mom? Are things okay there?"

He nodded. "A couple of days ago I went to see her. She's still trying to tell me more stuff, and I don't want to hear it. I know that I have to listen eventually. But other than that, we're fine."

She wanted to ask if she and Gage were fine, too. If making love had changed things forever, or if they could go back to their easy, teasing, fun relationship.

"I've missed you," she said before she could stop herself.

"I've missed you, too. More than I should."

Her heart skipped a beat and she felt positively giddy. Man, oh man, she had it bad.

"You ready?" he asked.

"Sure."

He stepped back, and she moved onto the porch, closing the door behind her. As they walked to the car, Gage rested his hand on the back of her neck. She liked the heat of him and the feel of his body close to hers. Unfortunately, there didn't seem to be much about Gage she didn't like.

They drove in silence to the motel. When they arrived, several parents were already pacing in the parking lot. Gage spoke to them, then went to the main office and collected keys from the night manager.

"Ready?" he asked Kari, as they walked up the stairs.

"No, but that's okay."

It was dark and quiet in the corridor. Voices from the parking lot faded as they moved toward the rear of the motel. Up ahead, light spilled out of an open door. The sound of laughter and loud voices drifted toward them.

"Do you do this sort of thing often?" she asked, trailing behind him.

"When asked. I prefer to come out at the request of the parents and clear things up before they get out of hand. That way I can get everyone home with a warning. If I get a call from the motel management, then it's official and I have to get tough. Most of the kids are mortified to be caught by me and their folks. They don't need much more encouragement to stop."

"For those who need more?"

"They'll be in trouble soon enough," Gage said, glancing at her as he paused near an open door. "Ready?"

She nodded, then braced herself for plenty of shrieking and tears. Gage stepped past the threshold and stalked toward the center of the room.

"Evening," he said calmly, as if he'd been invited.

Several teenagers screamed.

Kari followed him in. Kids were in various stages of undress. Two girls ducked into an adjoining room and quickly closed the door behind them. Two boys were brave enough, or drunk enough, to challenge Gage.

"We're not doing anything wrong, Sheriff," a skinny boy with dark hair said belligerently. "This is private property. You ain't got no right—"

Gage stood directly in front of the boy. "You talking to me, Jimmy?"

The teenager took a step back. His too-long hair hung in his eyes. He still wore a shirt and tie, although both were undone. The color faded from his face.

"Uh, yes, Sheriff. We've been quiet. We haven't made any trouble."

"That's good," Gage said evenly. "Your mama called me because she was real concerned. You're eighteen now, but your girlfriend is still only seventeen. Your mama was afraid you'd have a bit too much to drink and then things might get out of control."

Jimmy took another step back, which brought him in contact with the wall. "My mama called you?"

"Uh-huh. She's waiting downstairs in the parking lot."

One of the other boys snickered. Kari almost felt sorry for Jimmy.

Gage turned to those laughing. "Your mamas are here, too, boys. So let's all get dressed and head downstairs." He motioned to the adjoining room. "You want to see to the ladies?"

Kari nodded. She walked through the doorway and found herself in a living room. This must be the suite the Possum Landing Lodge was always advertising. The decorations were early tacky, with a gaudy red couch and fake oak coffee and end tables. Three velvet paintings decorated the walls.

"At least there's no Elvis," she said, passing a picture of dogs playing poker. She followed the sound of heated conversation.

"I can't believe this is happening," one girl said, as Kari entered the bedroom. "Tonight Jimmy and I were going to go all the way."

"Guess that will have to wait," Kari said, leaning against the door frame. "I realize you don't know me from a rock, but for what it's worth, my advice would be to make that very special occasion a little more private.''

Two girls, both young, pretty and blond, glared at her. She could read their minds. What could an old lady like Kari possibly know about having fun?

As Kari waited, they scrambled into dresses and high heels. When they hurried past her, she went to check the bathroom, where another girl sat on the floor. Her pale cheeks told their own story.

"You done being sick?" Kari asked.

The girl nodded and slowly got to her feet.

"Want some help?"

The teenager shook her head, then ran out of the bathroom. Kari turned to leave, then stared at the ice-filled bathtub. There had to be at least a dozen bottles of cheap liquor and wine chilling there.

"Great," she muttered, and went to find Gage.

She found him lecturing the last of the boys. The teenager escaped with a grumbled promise to think before acting next time.

"At least we got here in time," Gage said with a sigh as he closed the door of the suite. "All the girls gone?"

"Yes. One had been throwing up. She's not going to feel too great in the morning. Apparently, a big party was planned. There's a bathtub full of liquor in there."

He headed for the rest room. "Let's dump it, then we can head out of here."

"You don't want to keep any for yourself?" she

teased, as he bent down and grabbed a couple of bottles.

He glanced at the labels and shuddered. "My tastes have matured." His gaze slid to her. "In nearly everything."

She wasn't sure what he meant, but she liked that he finally seemed to have noticed she was there.

Gage poured while Kari handed him bottles. They worked quickly and soon the bathroom reeked of cheap liquor. It was only when they finished and moved back into the bedroom that he realized where he was.

The honeymoon suite.

The big round bed dominated the floor space, leaving little room for much more than a small dresser and a TV on a stand. Thick drapes kept out the night. The wood paneling had seen better days, as had the carpet. But eight years ago, Gage had thought this was just the place to secure his future with the woman he loved.

"What are you thinking?" Kari asked. "You have the strangest expression on your face."

He shrugged. "Ghosts."

"Ah. You liked to bring your lady friends here for a big seduction scene?"

"Not exactly. But I had planned to bring you here. I was going to propose, and after you said yes, I was going to make love to you."

Kari's smile faded. Several emotions skittered across her face, but he couldn't read them. Or maybe he didn't want to. Maybe it was better not to know what she was thinking. After all, she'd skipped town rather than marry him.

"You had it all planned out," she murmured.

"Down to the smallest detail, including proposing *before* we made love so you wouldn't think it was just about sex."

"I wouldn't have thought that. Not about you. I know the kind of man you are."

"Yeah, well..." He suddenly felt awkward and stupid for mentioning anything and headed for the door. But before he got there, Kari spoke again.

"Daisy and I practically had a fistfight over you in the produce aisle."

That brought him up short. "What are you talking about?"

She smiled. "Your wannabe girlfriend tried to warn me off. She said you weren't interested in me and that I could never have you back."

"What did you say?"

"A lot of things."

Which told him precisely nothing. Before he could figure out if he wanted to continue the conversation, she crossed to the nightstand and flipped on the clock radio. Tinny music filled the room. She fiddled with the knob until an oldies station came in, then crossed to stand in front of him.

"Dance with me," she said.

Then she was in his arms, and he found he didn't want to refuse her. Not when she felt so right pressed against him. Whatever might have gone wrong emotionally between them, physically they'd always been right together.

They moved together, swaying in time to the old ballad. He thought about what should have happened in this room all those years ago.

"I'm sorry you never got to your prom," he said, resting his cheek against her soft hair.

"Me, too. I would have liked to have those memories." She sighed. "I'm sorry I ran away. You were so good to me. I should have realized I could talk to you about anything—even being scared."

Past and present blurred. Gage closed his eyes. "Nothing is easy," he told her. "If I didn't know it before, I'm learning it now."

"Because of your mom?"

"Yeah. She loved her husband. I know she did. Yet there was this other man. She loved him, too, and I never figured it out. I want to be angry, but if she hadn't gone back to him, Quinn wouldn't exist."

"Sometimes life isn't as tidy as we would like."

He agreed with that. His life had changed forever. What had once been taken for granted wasn't a part of him anymore. A single piece of information had changed him forever. Changed him in a way that made everything else different.

He pulled Kari closer, enjoying the familiar heat of her body, the way she felt and the scent of her skin. Being with her allowed him to forget the issue of his father, for at least a short time. He could get lost in the past, in remembering something much sweeter. How he'd loved Kari more than he'd ever thought he *could* love someone. How he'd loved her long after she'd left, when he should have let go. The things he'd loved about her hadn't changed—her spirit, her generosity, her determination. She was the same woman—more mature, more experienced, but fundamentally the same.

The information could have been dangerous. Under other circumstances it would have been. If things were different he might think the reason he'd never been able to fall for anyone else was that he was a one-woman man and Kari was that woman. He might have worried about falling in love with her again.

But not anymore. Seeing her now, having her back in town, reminded him of all that might have been, but couldn't be now. Even if she wasn't leaving, they couldn't possibly be together. Everything was different now. Himself most of all.

"I'm glad we didn't get married," he said.

She raised her head and looked at him. "What are you talking about?"

Wasn't it obvious? "What if we'd married and had kids together? Eventually, I would have found out about my father."

"So?"

"It changes everything."

"Not for me. I feel badly that you're in pain and I want you to get your questions answered, but aside from that, it has no impact on anything. You're still the same man I knew eight years ago. If we'd married, you'd still be my husband and the father to my children. I would still love you."

Her blue eyes held his gaze. He could read her sincerity. She believed what she was saying, even if she was wrong.

"It changes everything," he said.

"You are the most stubborn man. I can't decide what to do with you."

Then she raised herself up on her toes and kissed him.

Chapter Thirteen

The soft pressure on his lips stunned Gage into immediate arousal. Need pulsed through him in waves that threatened to drown him in desire. Without thinking, he pulled her close and deepened the kiss, plunging his tongue inside her mouth, tasting her, teasing her, stroking her, *wanting* her.

She responded in kind, her body pressing against his, her hips against his arousal. She rubbed against him, as if they weren't close enough. When she closed her lips and sucked, he thought he was going to lose it right there.

"Oh, Gage," she breathed, making it clear that the heat wasn't being generated all on one side.

He'd made love with her enough times to know the joining would be spectacular, but not enough to have expectations of a sure thing. Kari's obvious interest excited and pleased him. She'd been a virgin their first time and he'd worried later that things hadn't gone well for her. Clearly, she'd decided she very much liked the act of making love. He started to back her toward the bed.

The bed. He raised his head and stared at the round mattress. How many times had he imagined them together here?

She turned and saw what had caught his attention. "Is it too weird to be here?"

"I don't know," he admitted.

"Do you want me to convince you, or just stop?"

He swung his gaze back to her. "Are you offering to seduce me?"

Color bloomed on her cheeks. She cleared her throat. "Yes, well, I'm not saying I could—just that if you were intrigued by the idea, I would be willing…" Her voice trailed off. "You did say you liked to watch."

Desire slammed into him like a truck going eighty. He didn't know why every single man in New York hadn't begged her to marry him, but somehow they'd missed the amazing jewel glittering in their midst. Somehow he, Gage, had gotten damn lucky.

Not only had Kari never been with another man before making love with him, but she was now offering to seduce him. As if he needed encouragement or persuasion.

He reached for her, determined to show her exactly what she did for him without even trying, when reality intruded.

"I don't have anything with me." He groaned. "Damn."

A slow smile teased her mouth. "Are we talking protection?"

He nodded.

Her smile broadened. "Our young friends might have been foolish about some things, but they were well prepared for others." She motioned to the television. "Exhibit A."

He turned and saw what he'd missed before. Sitting on top of the television was a jumbo box of condoms. There had to be at least a hundred inside.

"Somebody was planning on getting lucky in a big way," he said, pulling her back into his arms.

"Looks like it's going to be you."

"Looks like."

He lowered his head and kissed her. Despite the raging need inside him, he was determined to be gentle and take it slow. That mental promise lasted right up until Kari gently bit down on his tongue at the same time she slipped a hand between them and rubbed his arousal. He swore.

Kari shivered slightly at Gage's explicit language, but not out of shock. Instead she felt bone-melting need. She didn't know if it was the past intruding, or Gage's emotional vulnerability or her own emotional state, but something had happened tonight. Something that made her want to rip both their clothes off and make love to him.

She wanted to be taken. She wanted his body in hers, their hearts beating as one. She wanted the touching, the pleasure, the shared breath, the trembling aftermath. She wanted to bare her soul to him and stare down into the depths of his.

Her need made her bold in a way she'd never been before. When he jerked down the back zipper of her dress, she shrugged out of it as if she spent most of her day undressing in front of him. Before he could unfasten her bra, she did it for him. The scrap of lace slid to the floor. She brought his hands to her breasts, then gasped when she felt the heat of his touch. The ache between her thighs intensified as he cupped her curves while teasing her already tight nipples.

She reached for the buttons of his shirt while they kissed. Her fingers fumbled, but she kept at the task until she could rub her palms against the hair on his chest. From there she went to work on his belt, then his trousers. When she'd undone the zipper, she eased her hand inside his boxer shorts and wrapped her fingers around his hardness.

Such soft skin, she thought, deepening the kiss and beginning to move her hand. Soft skin around pulsing hardness. She eased back and forth, moving faster and faster until he caught her wrist and pulled her away.

"Not like that," he said with a smile.

She delighted in his confession—that she could have made him lose control with a simple touch.

While he stepped out of his shoes and pulled off his socks, she slipped off her panties. He continued to undress while she crossed to the condom box and removed one square packet. She turned to find Gage standing in the center of the room. He was naked.

She looked at him, from his dark eyes to his mouth, then to his chest, his flat belly and finally to his jutting maleness. He held out his hand for the condom. She handed it to him, then watched while he slipped it on.

When he moved to the bed, she followed. He stretched out on his back. "I thought you might like being on top," he said, his expression faintly wicked.

Kari thought about the position—her sliding up and down while he filled her. She thought about his hands on her body, touching, moving, stroking, delighting, and nearly stumbled in her eagerness.

She slid onto the bed, then stretched one leg over him. He filled her completely as she eased onto him.

He sucked in a breath, then instructed her not to move. "We need to get you caught up," he said, then proceeded to show her what he meant.

He touched her everywhere—from her ears to her breasts, down to her legs and between her thighs. He stroked the arc of curves, found secret places of delight and teased her into a frenzy. Tension filled her, making her want to ride him, but he held her back.

"Not yet," he whispered.

They kissed. He moved one hand to her nipples and tickled them until the pulsing inside her grew. Her thighs clenched and unclenched. Her breathing grew ragged. Finally, when she ached and perspiration dotted her back, he moved inside her.

She responded instantly, sliding up and down. On the first round trip, she felt herself falling off the edge. He made sure she went all the way by slipping his hand between her legs and rubbing her dampness until everything shattered.

Her climax overtook her, making her cry out. She

leaned forward, bracing her hands on the bed, riding him faster and faster, each up and down movement sending new waves of pleasure through her. She lost herself and didn't care about anything but her passion and her need.

There was more and more until nothing existed but the feel of him inside her. Then his hands settled on her hips, steadying her movements. His thrusts deepened as he collected himself. Kari forced her eyes open so she could watch her lover's release, only to find him watching her.

Then as he stiffened and called out her name, she saw down into his soul. For that one endless moment in time their hearts beat together. Then the pulsing of his climax carried her off on another mindless round of pleasure, and they lost themselves in the glory of their lovemaking.

When they finally disentangled, Kari expected Gage to roll away. He'd been distant from her ever since he found out about Ralph not being his biological father. But instead of sitting up or reaching for his clothes, he drew her close and wrapped his arms around her.

"Pretty amazing," he said quietly. "Even better than I'd imagined. And I'd imagined a lot."

"I know what you mean. I'm still trying to catch my breath."

He shifted so he was facing her, but kept an arm on her waist. "I haven't seen you in a few days."

She thought about explaining that it had actually

been a whole week, but didn't. "I've been working on the house. And you?"

"Work. Other stuff," he said casually.

"Is that getting better or worse?"

"About the same."

She wasn't sure she agreed with him. Not when he'd made the ridiculous statement about being glad they hadn't married and had children, based on some secret from the past.

"My mom came by for a visit," she said.

"How was that?"

"Weird, as always." She touched the line of his jaw, rubbing her fingers against his stubble. "I always had a very clear view of what happened when I was little. My parents went away and forgot about me. The fact that they kept my brothers with them only seemed to prove my point. But after talking with my mother, I'm not so sure."

She filled him in on the details of how she came to be left behind. "I saw my parents as the bad guys, but what was black and white is now gray. I still think they were wrong to leave me, but I can understand why they did what they did. I want to tell myself it doesn't affect anything, but it does. Still, the fact that my interpretation of the past might be different doesn't change my feelings. Am I making any sense?"

"Yes."

She stared into his dark eyes. "I guess my point is, I understand your confusion a little more clearly. Nothing is different for you, yet everything is different. Information changes perception—but does it change emotion? Am I less angry with my mother now that I know the circumstances that contributed to her decisions? I'm not sure.''

"Me, neither. About any of it."

She moved her hand to his mouth and traced his lips. "Don't you dare think you're anything but a wonderful man. You're the best man I've ever known."

"I doubt that."

"Don't. I'm telling the truth." She made an *X* above her left breast. "I swear."

"Thank you." He kissed her lightly.

Kari kissed him back. As she did, her words repeated themselves inside her head. Gage *was* the best man she'd ever known. He was everything any woman could want. He was...

Her chest tightened suddenly as she got it. The realization nearly made her laugh out loud. It also nearly made her cry.

She was in love with him. After all this time and all the miles she'd traveled, she was still in love with him.

Why hadn't she figured it out before? The clues had been there—her reaction to seeing him after all this time. Her willingness to make love with him after putting off other men. Her eagerness to spend time with him. The way she worried about him. Her ambivalence about looking for a teaching position in Dallas or Abilene.

"Kari? Are you okay?"

She nodded because speaking was impossible. Now what? What happened when one of her interviews led to a job offer? Did she hang around Possum Landing, hoping Gage would fall in love with her, too? He'd just said he was grateful they hadn't married. Hardly words to hang her dreams on.

The mature solution was to ask him about his feelings, to find out where things stood between them. She opened her mouth, then closed it. Not yet, she thought, burying her face in his shoulder. She needed a little time to get used to the idea of being in love with Gage.

"Hey," he said, stroking her back. "It's okay."

"I know," she lied, because she didn't know anything.

He kissed her head. "Want to come home with me and spend the night?"

She nodded. She loved him—there was nowhere else she would rather be.

Gage didn't have to work the next day, so they slept in late, then went over to her grandmother's house and set to work. They'd just started moving furniture out of the dining room, when there was a knock on the front door.

Kari went to answer it and found Edie waiting on the porch.

"Is Gage here?" his mother asked. "He wasn't home, but his truck is in the driveway, so I thought he might be helping you."

"Sure." Kari held open the front door, then called for Gage.

As she invited the older woman inside, she tried to quell the worry inside her. The past few hours had been magical. She and Gage had slept in each other's arms, only to awaken and make love again at dawn. Her feelings were still so new and tender that she didn't want anything to break the mood between them. Unfortunately, Edie's visit was bound to do just that.

Gage nodded at his mother. "What's going on?"

"You're avoiding me," Edie said bluntly. "I decided if you weren't going to come to me, I would chase you down myself. We need to talk."

Kari's throat went dry. "I'll go upstairs."

"No." Gage shot out a hand and grabbed her wrist. "You don't have to go." He gazed at her. "I'd prefer that you stay."

She nodded and led the way into the parlor. Edie perched on a chair, while Kari and Gage sat next to each other on the sofa.

"If you tell me that you're not really my mother, I'm going to be really pissed off," Gage said lightly.

Edie smiled slightly. "Sorry. You're stuck with me."

"I don't mind."

He reached for Kari's hand and laced their fingers together. She looked from him to his mom and wished this would all just go away.

"So here's the thing," Edie began. "When I went to Dallas the second time, I didn't know what I wanted or what I was feeling. Everything confused me. I just knew I had to see Earl one more time. Which I did. Obviously. Quinn is proof of that. But that's not all that happened."

Kari felt Gage brace himself against more bad news.

"We spent the night together. The next morning there was a knock on the hotel room door. A young woman stood there. She was barely eighteen." Edie shook her head. "She didn't look a day over fifteen, and she had two little babies with her. The second I saw her face, I knew the truth. Earl had been with her, as well. She'd brought her boys to meet their father."

Kari's stomach did a flip. She hadn't thought things could get worse, but she'd been wrong.

"Another conquest," Edie said bitterly. "I realized in that moment, that was all I'd been to him. Any feelings were on my side. I don't know how much of what he told me was truth and how much was lies. It didn't matter. What I had thought was love was infatuation. Or maybe it was just a justification to myself. If I thought I loved him, then sleeping with him didn't make me such a horrible person."

Tears filled her eyes. She blinked them away. Kari tightened her hold on Gage's hand. She was afraid to look at him. For once, she didn't want to know what he was thinking.

"What happened?" Gage asked, his voice low.

"The girl showed him the babies. He didn't deny they were his. He didn't do anything but get dressed and tell her he wished her well. That was it. No offer to marry her or even help out with his sons. I felt so stupid. The girl took off in tears. I ran into her in the lobby and found out her parents had thrown her and her two babies out the day she turned eighteen."

Gage wanted to run. He wanted to run so far and so fast that the words would be erased from his mind. He wanted to close his eyes and have the past disappear. But his mother kept talking, and he couldn't stop himself from listening.

But as she spoke an ugly thought appeared in his brain. This man—this Earl Haynes who used women and abandoned them—was an integral part of himself. Earl's biology was in Gage.

He thought of his own past, his inability to settle down with someone. How easily he moved from relationship to relationship. Was that because of his biological father? Was he a philanderer, too?

No! He didn't want that history, that blood, flowing through his veins. He didn't want to be a part of it.

But it was too late. The past had already occurred and he couldn't undo it. Not now.

Then, before he could make peace with any of it, his mother's words caught his attention.

"I couldn't leave her there alone," she was saying. "So I brought her home. We made up a dead husband and gave her a new last name."

Gage swore as the pieces all fell into place. Vivian Harmon was a close friend of the family. Her two sons, Kevin and Nash, were his age. Both tall, dark-haired, with dark eyes. And no father.

"Kevin and Nash?" he said.

She nodded. "Your half brothers. Vivian and I have talked about telling you four. We've gone back and forth a dozen times over the years. At first, I didn't want to say anything because of Ralph. He didn't want you to know. Vivian and I talked about it again after his death. At that point, I was too afraid to confess the truth. So I asked Vivian to keep quiet. She didn't mind. She'd married Howard years before and he'd been like a father to the boys. She never thought they were missing out.''

Gage felt as if the room were spinning. He didn't just have faceless half siblings in California, he had two right here in Texas. Not that Nash and Kevin lived here now. Nash was a negotiator with the FBI and Kevin was a U.S. Marshal, but they came home on occasion. He and Quinn had played with the twins all their lives. They'd double-dated, been on the same football and baseball teams, worked on each other's cars and shared their dreams with each other. Never had they considered the fact that they might share a whole lot more.

''Vivian's going to tell the boys,'' Edie said. ''Now that you're all going to know, it might help you four to talk about it.''

Gage wasn't sure what they were supposed to say. ''He has a family,'' he told her. ''Earl Haynes. I looked him up on the Internet. He's retired now, but he was a sheriff in a small town in California.''

His mother nodded slightly.

''There are other children. He has several sons from his first wife and a daughter by another woman.''

Edie winced. ''I suspected there was more family, but I wasn't sure.''

''You never asked.''

''I didn't want to know,'' she admitted.

At least she was being honest. "It's too much," he said.

"I'm sorry." She paused. "Do you have any other questions?"

"None that I can think of." He laughed humorlessly. "Just tell me that there aren't any other revelations."

"None that I'm aware of."

"Good."

He could live the rest of his life without any more secrets, he thought grimly.

Edie rose. "You haven't heard from Quinn yet, have you?"

"No. I'll let you know when he gets in touch."

Gage still didn't know how he was going to tell his brother the truth. Nor did he know how Quinn would react. It was a lot to take in.

He released Kari's hand, stood and walked his mother to the door. Tears filled her eyes.

"I'm sorry," she whispered.

He nodded and gave her a quick hug. When she'd left, he returned to the parlor.

Kari stood by the window. She turned to look at him. As they'd planned to work in the house, she wore a paint-spattered T-shirt and cutoffs. A scarf covered her hair, and she hadn't bothered with makeup. She still looked beautiful.

He wanted to go to her and hold her so tightly that he couldn't tell where one ended and the other began. He wanted to breathe in the scent of her and return to that place where he'd felt everything was going to be all right. Unfortunately, that time had passed.

"I know I said I'd help, but I need to head out and—" He broke off, not knowing what he had to do. He only knew that he needed to be by himself for a while.

"It's okay," she said. "I understand."

"I'll be in touch."

"You said that before."

Had he? "This time I mean it. I'll call you tonight."

He walked to the front door and let himself out. He crossed to his own yard and was about to climb the front porch steps, when he heard her calling his name. He turned.

"What's up?" he asked.

She crossed the driveway to stand next to him. "This is wrong," she said, determination blazing in her eyes. "I know you're going through a lot right now, but you can't let it destroy everything."

"What are you talking about?"

She swallowed. "Last time, I was the one to walk away. It looks like this time you're going to walk away. Do you think we'll ever get it right?"

Chapter Fourteen

Gage felt as if he'd been turned to stone. He couldn't move, couldn't speak. Then the sensation passed and he was able to draw in a breath.

Do you think we'll ever get it right?

"What the hell are you talking about?" he demanded.

Kari didn't back down from his obvious temper. Instead, she planted her hands on her hips and glared back at him.

"I'm talking about us. You and me. There's something here, Gage. I know you can feel it. Lord knows, it's keeping me up at night. Eight years ago I panicked. I was too young to tell you I needed time, so I ran. My fears and my desire to experience my dreams kept us apart. I've grown up and you've changed, too, yet whatever we had is still alive. But I'm afraid that this time your past is going to rip us apart.''

He didn't know what to say. While he was willing to admit there was something between Kari and himself, he'd never thought past the moment. He knew about her plans, and they didn't include him. He'd been okay with that. Now she was suddenly changing the rules.

''Are you saying you're not leaving Possum Landing?'' he asked, not sure how he felt about any of this.

''I'm saying I don't know. Last night you told me you were glad we'd never married and had children. You said the fact that Ralph isn't your biological father changes everything.''

''It does.'' How could it not?

She dropped her hands to her sides and took a deep breath. ''See, that's what I'm afraid of. I want you to see that it doesn't matter.''

His temper erupted. ''You're ignoring the obvious. I understand that Ralph Reynolds had a tremendous influence on my life. He raised me to believe certain things and to act a certain way, but those are only influences. What about my basic character? Were you listening to what my mother said about Earl Haynes? He got a seventeen-year-old girl pregnant. When he found out about her twins, he simply walked away. That is my heritage. That is the character of the man who fathered me. I have to live with that and make peace with it, if possible. I may not know much about him, but I know he was a cheating bastard who wouldn't take responsibility for his own children. I'm not willing to take a chance on passing those qualities on. Are you?''

Pain flashed through her blue eyes. Her mouth trembled. "You're not him," she said softly. "You're not him."

"Are you willing to bet your children's future on that?"

"Yes," she said with a confidence that stunned him. "I know you. I've known you for years. You're the kind of man who would put his life on the line for his town because he doesn't know another way to do things. You're the kind of man who looks after other people's grandmothers, and cares for his own mother when her husband dies. You're responsible, caring, gentle, loving and passionate. You're a good man."

Her words hit him like arrows finding their way to his soul. "You don't know what the hell you're talking about," he said, turning away.

She grabbed his arm and stepped in front of him. "I know exactly what I'm saying. You are the same man you were last month and last year. Believing anything else is giving power to a ghost. I believe in you with all my heart."

She stopped talking and pressed a hand to her mouth. Tears filled her eyes. "Oh, Gage."

He watched her warily.

She blinked the tears away. "I just realized, it doesn't matter how much I believe in you. If you won't believe in yourself, there's no point in having this conversation. I can't convince you. I can't make you believe. And loving you won't matter because you won't let it.''

He froze. ''What did you say?''

She lowered her hand. ''I love you. I'm beginning to think I never stopped. You still have every quality I loved before, but you're even better now. How was I supposed to resist that?''

Her words stunned him. She loved him? Now? ''I don't believe you,'' he said flatly.

''I'm not surprised. Worse, I don't know how to convince you. I'm beginning to think I don't know anything.'' She sighed and took a step back, holding out her hands, palms up.

''I love you and I'm terrified you're going to let me walk away because of some ridiculous obsession with the past and what it means to you today. I'm afraid we're going to lose our second chance, and I'm willing to bet there won't be a third.''

Kari's declaration had caught him off guard. Defenseless and confused, he wanted to retreat. *No more words,* he thought. *No more.*

But she wasn't finished. ''It all comes down to making choices,'' she said. ''Are you willing to trust yourself?'' She gave a strangled laugh. ''I guess that's *your* most significant question. Mine is different. Do you still love me? Are you interested in any of this? I've been going on, based on the assumption that my feelings matter to you—and they may not. But if they do, it's your choice. Are you willing to let the biology rule your life? You do have a choice in this.''

She turned away and started for her house. When she reached the driveway, she glanced back at him.

"Let me know what you decide. I hope you have enough sense to see how lucky we are to have found each other again. I think we could be wonderful together. At one time I was set on leaving Possum Landing, but that's not an issue anymore. What I don't know is if you can get past everything you've learned recently. One way or the other, I have to make a decision. To stay or go. When you figure out what you want, let me know."

And then she was gone. Gage stared after her, watching her disappear into the house, feeling his lifeblood flow away.

She loved him.

After all these years, after all the waiting—he'd just realized that's what he'd been doing—she finally realized she loved him. She'd come to the same conclusion he had—that all they'd loved about each other was still in place, only better.

The information came a couple of weeks too late.

He might want to be with Kari with all his heart, but did that matter? He had nothing to offer her. Without a past he could depend on, he had no future.

Kari walked into the house to find the phone ringing. At first she thought about ignoring it. There was no way that Gage could have run inside and called her. Besides, if he had something he wanted to say, he would simply come over and tell her.

So she let the machine get it. But when a woman identified herself as someone from the Abilene school where she'd interviewed, she grabbed the receiver.

"Hello?"

"Kari?"

"Yes."

"Hi! This is Margaret Cunningham. We spoke during your interview?"

"I remember. How are you?" Kari wiped the tears from her face.

"Great. I have wonderful news. We were all so impressed, and I'm delighted to be calling you with a job offer."

Kari wasn't even surprised. Of course this would happen moments after she made her declaration to Gage. Fate was nothing if not ironic.

She listened while the other woman gave details about the job, including a starting salary and when they would like her to start. Kari wrote it all down and promised to call back within forty-eight hours. When she'd hung up, she grabbed a pillow from a nearby chair and sent it sailing across the room.

"Dammit, Gage," she yelled into the silence. "Now what? You're not going to tell me what I want to hear, are you. And if you are, you'll take your time, and then what am I supposed to do? I told you I loved you. Doesn't that mean anything?"

She wanted to stomp her feet, as well, but figured that was immature and wouldn't help. She hurt inside. Probably because she'd done the right thing at last and declared her feelings, only to have Gage not respond to them. He'd listened and then had let her walk away. Not exactly the sign of a man overwhelmed by loving feelings.

She sank onto the chair and covered her face with her hands. That's what was really wrong, she thought sadly. She'd admitted she loved Gage and he hadn't offered her love in return. He hadn't offered her anything.

Over the next twenty-four hours, Kari alternately cried, ate ice cream, threw unbreakable objects and slept. She also hovered by the phone, willing it to ring.

When it did, she found herself being offered another job, this one in the Dallas area.

Sometime close to noon the next day, while she cried her way through a shower, she finally got it. It was as if the heavens had opened and God had spoken to her directly.

She couldn't force Gage to love her back and she couldn't insist he live on her timetable. The only control she had was over herself. Her feelings, her goals, her life. Gage was his own person. He had to make the decisions that were right for him.

The realization left her feeling very much alone. What did she do now? Did she keep her life on hold, hoping he would come to terms with everything and realize that they belonged together? Or did she move on, aware that he might never come around?

After her shower, she dressed and fussed with her hair. She applied makeup, then headed out the door.

She found Gage at the sheriff's station. He was talking with one of the deputies, so Kari waited until they were finished. When Gage was alone in his office, she slipped inside and closed the door behind her.

He looked tired. Dark shadows stained the skin under his eyes. While she couldn't read his thoughts, she felt he looked a little wary. No doubt he feared her next confession.

"About yesterday," she said, settling into a chair across from his desk. She really wanted to pace, but figured if she stayed standing, he would, as well. Although the closed door gave them the illusion of privacy, in reality Gage's office walls were glass. Anyone could watch what was going on. Better to have things appear calm. At least no one could hear the thundering of her heart.

"Kari," Gage began, but she held up her hand to stop him.

"I'd like to go first," she said quickly.

He hesitated, then nodded.

Every cell in her body screamed at her to run to him and beg him to say he loved her. She desperately wanted him to sweep her up in his arms, hold her close and swear he would never let her go. She wanted him to declare his love with a sincerity and passion that would keep her tingling for the rest of her life.

Instead, she was going to tell him it was okay for him to let her go.

"I was wrong yesterday," she said. "I shouldn't have confessed my feelings. Or if I did, I should have done it differently. Nothing about this situation is your fault. You have so much going on right now and I just added to your load. For me this is huge, but for you it's just one more piece of the puzzle."

She forced herself to smile and hoped it came out even borderline normal. "You need time to figure out what's going on. You have a lot to come to grips with. I'm not saying I don't love you. I do. I can't imagine life without you. But I'm not going to force myself on you. You need time, and I'm going to give you that.''

Now came the tricky part. She swallowed and twisted her fingers together. ''So, to that end, I'm accepting a job in Abilene. It's close enough that if you change your mind—'' She cleared her throat. ''It would be doable until my school year ended. And if you decide this is… I mean, if I'm not what you want, then I'll be getting on with my life.''

He looked as if she'd sucker punched him. ''Kari, don't.''

''Don't what? Leave? Isn't it the right thing to do?''

He shook his head. She had a bad feeling he'd meant ''Don't love me.''

Pain gripped her. She forced herself to go on. ''Just to keep things from being too awkward, I've hired someone to finish the work on the house. The property management company will take care of selling it. So I'm heading out in the morning. I wanted to tell you that, too. Goodbye, I mean.''

''You don't have to leave because of me.''

It hurt to breathe. He was saying he shouldn't be the reason she left—not ''Don't go.''

''There's nothing to keep me here,'' she said, forcing herself to breathe in and out. The pain would pass eventually. Life would go on. This wouldn't kill her, no matter how it felt right now.

''My family, such as it is, lives elsewhere. With

my grandmother gone, Possum Landing isn't home anymore. She was always the one who mattered. My mother might have given birth to me, but my grandmother was the keeper of my heart while I was growing up.'' She stood slowly.

There was so much more she wanted to say—but what was the point? Obviously her love was one-sided. Not the haven she had wanted it to be. If only…

''Goodbye, Gage,'' she said finally.

Gathering every ounce of courage and strength, she turned and walked out of his office. She didn't look back, not even once. She'd done the right thing. When she'd begun to heal in, oh, fifty years or so, she could be proud of that. Right now, she just wanted to be anywhere but here.

Gage watched her go. With each step she took, he felt a piece of his soul crumble to dust.

She was leaving. She'd said as much and he believed her. Under the circumstances, it would be best for both of them. She would get on with her life and he would try to figure out who he was now that he was no longer one of five generations of Reynolds, born and bred in Possum Landing.

He turned to his computer screen, but the small characters there didn't make any sense. Instead of words, he saw Kari leaving. Again. He'd let her go the first time because she'd deserved to have a chance at her dreams. This time he was letting her go because…

Because it was the right thing to do. Because she deserved more than he had to offer. Because—

He swore as her words echoed inside him. While Aurora was her mother, she wasn't the keeper of Kari's heart. Her grandmother had been that. For Kari, Aurora was nothing more than biology. No yesterdays bound them together. No shared laughter, no talks late at night, no Christmas mornings.

Gage curled his hands into fists as a kaleidoscope of memories rushed through his brain. His father teaching him to ride a bike, then, years later, to drive a car. His father taking him fishing. Just the two of them, leaving town several hours before dawn for a camping trip. Long walks, evenings by the fire building models. Frank conversations about women and sex—Ralph Reynolds had admitted knowing less about the former than the latter. His father had taught him to tell the truth, be polite, think of others. He'd taught Gage respect and courage.

Earl Haynes might have given Gage life, but Ralph Reynolds had made sure that life meant something.

Gage stood up with a force that sent his chair sailing across the room. He raced to the door and out toward the front of the building. He might not have all the answers, but he knew one thing for sure—he wasn't going to lose Kari a second time. Not if she was willing to take a chance on him.

He pushed open the front door and saw her on the sidewalk. "Kari," he called. "Wait."

She turned. He saw tears on her beautiful face. Tears and an expression so lost and empty that it nearly broke his heart. Then she saw him. And as he watched, hope struggled with pain.

"Don't go," he said when he reached her side. He

wrapped his arms around her. "Please, don't go. I can't lose you again."

He cupped her face and stared into her eyes. "Kari, I love you. I've always loved you. I didn't want to admit it, even to myself, but I've been waiting for you to come back. Don't go."

A smile played around her mouth. It blossomed until she beamed at him.

"Really? You love me?"

"Always."

"What about what your mother told you?"

"I don't have all the answers."

Her smile never wavered as love filled her eyes, chasing away the tears. "You don't have to. We'll figure them out together. No matter what, I'll be here for you."

That was all he wanted to hear. He kissed her. "I love you. Stay. Please. I know you have to work in Abilene for a year. That's what you agreed to, right? We'll work it out. I want to be with you. I want to marry you and have babies with you."

She laughed. "I haven't accepted the job yet. I was going to go home and call right now. I guess I'll have to tell them no."

He couldn't believe she would do that for him. He pulled her close again and pressed his face into her soft hair. "I never want to lose you again."

"You won't. I'll marry you, Gage. And we'll have those babies. When you figure out what you want to do about your half siblings in California, we'll deal with that, as well."

He raised his head and looked at her. Love filled

him, banishing the shadows and making everything right. "How did I get so lucky?"

"I could ask the same thing. My answer is that I love you. After all this time, you're still the one."

*   *   *   *   *

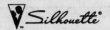

SPECIAL EDITION™

Coming in August 2002,
from Silhouette Special Edition and

CHRISTINE RIMMER,

the author who brought you the popular series

CONVENIENTLY YOURS,

brings her new series

THE SONS OF CAITLIN BRAVO

Starting with

HIS EXECUTIVE SWEETHEART
(SE #1485)...

One day she was the prim and proper executive assistant...
the next, Celia Tuttle fell hopelessly in love with her boss,
mogul Aaron Bravo, bachelor extraordinaire. It was clear he
was never going to return her feelings, so what was a girl to
do but get a makeover—and try to quit. Only suddenly,
was Aaron eyeing his assistant in a whole new light?

And coming in October 2002, MERCURY RISING,
also from Silhouette Special Edition.

**THE SONS OF CAITLIN BRAVO: Aaron, Cade and Will.
They thought no woman could tame them.
How wrong they were!**

Where love comes alive™

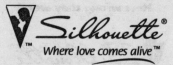

$ Saving Money $
Has Never Been
This Easy!

Just fill out and send in this form from any
October, November and December 2002 books
and we will send you a coupon booklet worth a
total savings of $20.00 off future purchases of
Harlequin and Silhouette books in 2003.

Yes! It's that easy!

**Where royalty and romance
go hand in hand...**

The series finishes in

with these unforgettable love stories:

THE ROYAL TREATMENT
by Maureen Child
October 2002 (SD #1468)

TAMING THE PRINCE
by Elizabeth Bevarly
November 2002 (SD #1474)

ROYALLY PREGNANT
by Barbara McCauley
December 2002 (SD #1480)

Available at your favorite retail outlet.

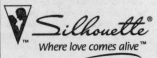

COMING NEXT MONTH

SSECNM1102

SPECIAL EDITION